Greenways

David Reynolds-Moreton

sci-fi-cafe.com

Introduction

There are three stories that were written to form a loose series called The *Sapient Continuum - Transplant*, *Greenways* and *The Tribe* (formerly known as *The Inosculation Syndrome*). Purists would read them in that order, but Reynolds-Moreton has crafted his tales so cleverly that they can be read in any order. Fans of prequels might enjoy reading *The Tribe* first. The astute reader may even find nods to this series in his other books, of which we're proud to publish over twenty at the time of writing this introduction.

One:
The Invitation

Kᴇʟ ᴡᴀs ᴛʀᴏᴛᴛɪɴɢ nimbly along the well worn pathway in the middle of one of the main branches, occasionally glancing upwards to look for whip tendrils when he saw something move on the path ahead. He stopped dead in mid stride.

This sudden halt was almost automatic through years of training and realizing the possible consequences of not doing so when confronted by the unexpected.

Just ahead of him, the pathway was brightly illuminated by a shaft of light from the Greater Sun, which had somehow filtered down through the dense green canopy overhead and the path looked normal enough, but something had moved on the surface of the track, and that didn't usually happen.

He had only caught a glimpse of movement, a mere twitch of the surface, but that was enough to tell him that all was not as it appeared to be.

Kel moved a little closer to the suspect portion of the pathway but couldn't see anything out of the ordinary, except perhaps a tiny crack in the worn surface of the bark which covered the mighty branch.

He should have been carrying his stave with him as they all did when away from the group, but as it was only a short journey to the Story Teller's cave, so he hadn't bothered this time.

Kel broke a small twig off a nearby bough to act as a marker on the pathway, and then went back up the track to where he knew there was a stave plant growing in the crotch of a side branch.

The stave plant had to be treated with a fair amount of caution, as the juice from its severed end was deadly if left in contact with the skin for any length of time, so a little ritual had been devised to protect the stave gatherers from the deadly liquid.

From the outer edge of the main clump Kel selected a stave of the right length for what he had in mind, and withdrew his lesser cutting knife from its pouch on his belt. Very carefully he made a deep incision around the base of the bamboo like stave, making sure that his feet were as far away from the plant as possible while still maintaining his balance in a crouching position.

Having completed the encircling cut, he gathered up several handfuls of assorted leaves which had accumulated at the bottom of the plant, and pressed them around the now oozing cut on the stave, making very sure he didn't allow any of the corrosive juice to get on his hands. Reaching up into the clump, he then pulled off two of the long ribbon like leaves from the stave plant and bound the leaves into a loose pad encompassing the cut at the base of the stem.

Taking a firm grip on the stave at shoulder height, Kel now rocked the stem back and forth and from side to side, the milky white juice spurting harmlessly out into the pad of leaves and trickling down the remainder of the stem, eventually no doubt to be reabsorbed by the plant, for nothing went to waste in the forest.

When it looked as though all the deadly sap had been drained from the stem, he repositioned his grip and bent it down towards the surface of the main branch on which he stood, throwing all his weight behind the last thrust as the stave came level.

There was a sharp crack, and the stave was now free, but the end was still covered in the sticky thick milk-like fluid and so was not safe for him to use as yet.

Positioning the base of the new stave between his feet and turning it slowly, Kel allowed a small trickle of his urine to run down to the cut end, which he held just above the surface of the pathway.

Someone, a long time ago, had discovered quite accidentally no doubt, that the uric acid in urine reacted with the plant juice, converting it into a hard and harmless resinous substance and so the ritual of stave manufacture had been passed on down through the generations to the present day, although the actual chemistry of the process would have been well beyond their understanding.

Slowly the milky-white fluid on the end of the stave began to thicken, turning a pale honey brown colour, and while the hardening process continued, Kel got to thinking of the day when he would be presented with the Greater Cutting Knife, a sure sign of manhood and a place of respect within the group.

As far as he could make out, there were only a few more cycles of the lesser sun to bring him up to the age of manhood, and then he would have a proper long-bladed cutting knife, a truly fearful weapon.

The cutting knives were the group's most treasured possessions, and responsibility for their safe keeping was drummed in at an early age and then reinforced again later when the coming of age ceremony was held.

Kel had been on his way to the Story Teller, hoping to learn about one of the lesser stories, the one about the cutting knives, when the journey had been interrupted by the bark moving on the pathway.

The blob of resinous compound on the end of the stave had now turned a dark brown colour and hardened, and it was at this point that Kel knew it was safe to use the stave as the juice within it had been rendered harmless.

He needed some bait to put on the stave to tempt whatever it was underneath the pathway to show itself, and to this end he looked around for a large fruiting body or seed pod to adorn the end of the stave with.

As Kel made his way back to the marker twig he had left on the main branch, he noticed a large purple globe, about the size of his head, hanging down from a vine over one of the side branches. It wasn't one of the normal food fruits, and he couldn't recall having seen one like it before, so this too must be treated with a degree of caution.

Leaving the main branch, he went along the side spur and then climbed up a lesser bough so that he was level with his target. Wrapping both legs tightly around the branch, he leaned out and gave the purple pod a poke with his stave. It just swung back and forth on its long thin stem, slowly coming to rest again after a short while. It hadn't emitted a swarm of angry insects, which some pods did, nor did it squirt out any noxious fluid to warn off anything wishing to use it for a meal.

Increasing his grip on the branch, Kel lined the stave up with the pod and stabbed at it firmly, aiming for the point where it joined the vine from which it hung. The first attempt was unsuccessful, causing the pod to swing wildly to and fro, narrowly missing his head.

As the pod swung back out of his reach, he noticed a strange smell, almost like that of an animal which had died many days ago.

Maybe this was the defence which the pod used to prevent it from being eaten he thought, but then some of the strange creatures of the forest seemed to prefer old carcasses to a fresh kill.

As this was a new discovery, there would be much to learn from it, and he would report any details he could gather to his group upon returning.

A second stab at the pod produced better results, and as the pod swung away from him, now captive on the end of the stave, he was nearly pulled off the branch.

Gently Kel pulled the stave towards him, and as the pod drew nearer, the smell increased to the point where he wrinkled his nose in disgust at the aroma of rotting meat.

There was no way he would touch the purple pod with his hands until he knew a little more about it, so he drew it as near to him as the hanging vine would allow, and then jammed the stave between the branch on which he sat and his body.

Carefully reaching out with the lesser knife in his hand, Kel severed the pod from its supporting stem, and was nearly catapulted from his perch as the full weight of the pod came onto the end of the stave as it bent down under the unexpected load.

He could feel the roughness of the bark cutting into his legs as he increased his grip still further to prevent himself from being spun round underneath the bough, and grimaced at the searing pain.

After he had regained his balance, Kel slowly drew the stave toward him, sliding it beneath his body bit by bit, the noxious odour of the pod getting stronger as it came ever nearer to his twitching nostrils.

By the time he had the pod within hands reach, he realized that he had been holding his breath, and let it out with a great whoosh, only to refill his lungs with the overpowering stench of something long since dead.

Regaining his feet, Kel drove the stave a little deeper into the smelly pod to make sure it didn't slip off, and then began the journey back to the marker twig to see what lay beneath the suspect area of pathway.

There had been various rumours for some time now of a new creature in the area, something which lived under the surface of the branches and grabbed its prey as it passed by overhead.

Two people of the neighbouring group had been lost this way, disappearing down a hole which had opened up in a branch and then seemed to cover itself up again, leaving no trace of what had happened. Things were forever changing in the forest, and not always for the better.

Kel wondered if the twitching bark on the pathway was the home of one such creature, although none had been spoken of it in their area of the forest.

With great care he approached the suspect part of the branch, and then pushed the pod on the end of his stave towards the area of the bark which had twitched earlier. With the purple fruit positioned directly over the faint line in the surface, Kel stood waiting for some sort of reaction, ready to leap backwards if it should happen too near him.

Perhaps he had been mistaken and there wasn't anything under the bark after all. He was about to give up the idea of tempting whatever it was under the pathway to show itself, for nothing untoward had happened for several minutes, and then it did, and with a suddenness which took him completely by surprise.

The bark of the huge branch had burst open with a soft ripping sound, the two halves of a trapdoor springing inwards while a grey shiny tentacle whipped out wrapping itself around the purple pod and stripping it off the end of the stave so quickly that Kel hardly felt the jerk. The two halves of the door to the creature's hiding place snapped shut in the same instant that the pod disappeared, and all was still again.

It had all happened so quickly that Kel didn't even have a chance to step back, so it was just as well that he was outside the range of the creature when it struck the pod. He still had his stave, and as it was about four times as long as he was high, he thought it would probably be safe enough to tap the trapdoor to see if the creature would appear again.

Kel tapped and banged on the trapdoor for all he was worth, but got no response from the creature within. Maybe it was still eating the pod, or the pod had poisoned it.

There was only one thing left to do before reporting the event to the rest of the group, and so he took the marker pod from his belt and rubbed it in a large circle around the area of the trapdoor, a warning to all to be on guard against possible danger.

The marker pods were a recent find for the group, and although they had only been in use for a relatively short period of time, had proved their worth many times over.

They grew in an area which was shared by Kel's group and the next nearest one in the forest, and when it was found that they were no use as a food source, someone had discovered that if they were rubbed hard on a rough surface, the juice which exuded from them dried a deep red colour and was ideal as a warning mark for anything dangerous.

Everyone now carried one of the new marker pods, and little red marks were appearing on rotten branches, dangerous fruits and plants, and now suspect areas of bark on the main trackways would also be marked.

Life was getting a little safer now, but then new hazards were springing up out of nowhere every now and again, so all in all, some sort of balance was maintained by nature.

Kel continued his journey to the Story Teller's cave in one of the mighty tree trunks which reared up from the forest floor to the dizzying heights above, wondering if the wise old man would be able to shed any light on the new threat to the group.

He looked up as something above him screamed. Very few people had ever gone all the way up to the top of the forest, as it took such a long time to climb up to the sky, and there were all sorts of new hazards along the way.

They had quite enough trouble dodging the perils of their own level without getting used to new ones at other layers in the great forest complex. Also, the light from the greater sun was far too bright for most of those who had made the effort and reached the top of the forest as it hurt their eyes, so it wasn't a popular place to go.

The forest floor was a very long way down, and almost as dark during the day, as the night was at the level in which the group lived when the lesser sun failed to rise, which it did at regular intervals. Also the lower one went, the wetter it got, and at ground level there were large pools of water which, according to the Story Teller, contained huge creatures that were always hungry for anything which wandered or fell their way.

Kel spent as much time as he could at the Story Teller's cave, fascinated by the tales of the past and the strange monsters which lived at the different levels in the forest.

There were the greater tales, telling of the group's major events through time, the stories of the greater and lesser sun, the litany of foods which were safe to eat, creatures to avoid and the general laws of the group.

The lesser tales were more specific, dealing with a single item, and it was the tale of the greater and lesser cutting knives which Kel wanted to hear again.

As he neared the cave of the Story Teller, Kel took extra care as this was an area well known for its propensity of whip tendrils, and although many of them had been cut down to make it safe for those travelling along the great branch highway, more could well have grown since the last cutting.

Kel remembered the story told of the time before they had the cutting knives, and how their movements were very restricted as the tendrils somehow seemed to sense that moving food was around and grew in huge numbers.

Before the time of the knives, if anyone was caught by a tendril that was the end of them. But now, if you acted quickly enough, the first tendril to wrap around you could be cut, and if you were lucky and didn't fall to the forest floor, you lived to tell the tale, although many in their enthusiasm to rid themselves of the dreaded creepers cut themselves at the same time, and then suffered a slow death from the fungus which seemed to grow very rapidly in open wounds.

No one knew for sure if the whip tendrils were animal or vegetable, but it was thought they were some type of animal as they moved so quickly, whereas most plant creatures were slower in their movements, but made up for their lack of rapid response in the cunning way they set their traps.

The Story Teller lived apart from the main group, but no one knew why and few had ever thought to ask him. He was held in some reverence as his knowledge of medicinal plants and what could be eaten was paramount to the group's survival, and without this they would not continue as a race for very long.

The story telling was just entertaining for most, but held a strange fascination for the ever curious Kel, and he never tired of listening to the old legends of the past and how things had come about.

The cave in the main trunk of the giant tree was part natural, it was thought, and part made by previous Story Tellers. It had a main room and several smaller side rooms in which food and the tools of his trade were stored.

Although the Story Teller didn't look all that old, the oldest member of the group maintained that he had looked just the same when he had been a youth, so the Story Teller's age was something of an enigma to those few who ever bothered to think about it.

Kel often wondered what would happen to the group if a misfortune befell the Story Teller, as there was no one else to take his place and his knowledge would die with him. He didn't like to mention this to him in case it somehow brought about the feared disaster, and he had a sneaky feeling that he would be offered the job if he did, and that wasn't what he wanted to do with his life.

The branch on which Kel now stood had broadened out where it joined the vast main trunk as it soared ever upwards to the sky above.

It was here that the Story Teller grew his little garden of special plants which were used to treat the ills of the group, not that they were taken ill very often, but when they did, it was usually fatal unless treated quickly.

He remembered once as a child being brought here by an elder, and being made to drink some foul concoction to cure a fever, not that he could remember the fever itself, but the memory of the medicine remained.

Stepping carefully on the narrow clearway between the plants, Kel made his way to the entrance of the cave and called Mec by name, being one of very few in his group who had that honour.

'Come in young man,' the Story Teller replied, 'I thought you might be along soon, so I've made some food ready, and I have a little surprise for you as well.'

Kel stepped into the gloom of the tree cave, careful not to tread on a series of little pots which littered the floor and made his way over to Mec, the Story Teller, who was bent over a bench against the far wall of the cave.

'What's the surprise you have for me?' asked Kel, always eager to learn of anything new.

'That, you will have to wait for. We will eat first while I tell you what I've been doing, and why.'

Mec lead the way into one of the smaller side caves, and motioned Kel to sit down on a stool made from a large gourd. Before him was an array of fruits which he knew well, some of which were quite rare and considered a great delicacy among the group, and here they were in plenty, together with some he had never seen before.

'I've laid on a little feast for you to celebrate my latest discovery, which one day you will find of great use, no doubt.' Mec sat himself down opposite Kel, and began passing the bowls of delicacies to him, Kel taking one each of those which took his fancy, but avoiding the ones he wasn't familiar with out of sheer habit.

'When you have had your fill of those you have chosen, I would like you to try one of these.' said Mec, showing Kel a wizened black-coloured berry.

'It may not look much, but it may save your life one day. I have lived the whole of one cycle of the lesser sun on one of these berries per day, together with a little water, and I feel well and full of energy, as usual. If you were thinking of making a long journey, and were not sure of what food to eat, then a few of these may well save you from losing your strength, or even starving.'

Was this the surprise Mec said he had in store? Kel didn't think much of it, and was a little disappointed. He was eager to get on with the story telling, as he had a lot of questions to ask, and each of them would need a story to provide the full answer he thought.

'All right Mec, I'll try your new black fruit now.' said Kel, a little impatiently, having eaten his fill and eager to get it done with and on to more important things. After all, it was the wonderful stories he had come to hear, not mess about tasting some ugly black fruit-like thing which probably tasted foul anyway.

'First, watch this.' said Mec, picking up one of the black berries and dropping it into a small gourd of water. The black wrinkled sphere swelled up the instant it hit the water, and very soon filled the little gourd, all the water having been absorbed into the fruit which was now like a firm skinned deep purple ball.

'Take it out and taste it,' invited Mec, 'it's quite harmless and you'll be surprised at what you find.'

Kel did as he was bid, and took a tentative bite out of the purple sphere. His eyes opened wide as the sweet thick juice trickled down from the corners of his mouth and the flavours exploded on his palette. Flavours? Yes, there were many of them, running one into the other as the juice ran back down his throat, touching the different areas of his taste buds.

'Well, that's a pleasant surprise.' said Kel, eagerly taking another bite out of the glistening sphere.

'You will notice that you could carry quite a lot of them in a small bag hung from your waist belt, and yet they would provide you with many days worth of good nourishing food, that's if you can find the water to go with them, and that's usually possible.' Mec sat back on his stool with a pleased smile on his face.

'Now that's only one of the surprises I have in store for you, the other one will take a little explaining. Do you remember the tale of the forest floor, and how dark it is?'

'Yes,' said Kel, 'that's one of the stories I wanted you to tell me about again.'

'Well, you don't know why we need to go down there at the moment, so I'll have to explain that, but down there we have to go, sometimes. We have to wait at the lowest level for some little while to get our eyes accustomed to the very faint light'. Mec paused to sample another of the black shiny fruits he was so pleased with.

'During that time we are vulnerable to being attacked by whatever thinks we are good for a meal, so if we could see a little better we would stand a better chance of surviving.

'I had noticed that some of the strange flying creatures sometimes give out a light to attract one another and some fungi also glow in the dark when the lesser sun is absent. I have been collecting some of these things which glow in the dark, and extracting the juices from them. It has taken a long time, but I have now found that by mixing certain juices together, they too will glow in the dark, and at the time of the lesser sun not giving us light, I found that I could see quite well to walk around safely once my eyes got used to the low light level.'

Kel looked surprised at the idea of being able to make light, and asked to see it actually working.

'Be patient, young man, and you shall see it, and one day may even use it to guide your way in dark places. I have reduced the juices to a dried powder, so all you have to do is add a little of each powder to some water, shake it up a little, and you have light!. Here, let me show you, I can see you are bursting with curiosity.' Mec got up from his seat with an ill concealed chuckle and went into another of the little rooms which went around the wall of the main cave.

'Here, you can do it yourself. Take a little of that powder and some of that one, and drop them into that insect body case. You can see that the case of the insect is transparent, so if we can make light inside it, the light will come through the casing. Good, now add a little water and shake it up.

'There, you see, it glows. How well can you see in here if I stand in the opening blocking out the external light?'

Kel let his eyes get used to the gloom, and was surprised to be able to see details of the little room slowly getting better and better.

'This is wonderful,' said Kel, 'I can see quite well. We shall be able to see to go about the walkways when the lesser sun fails to shine now.'

'No you won't,' said Mec, 'this is to be kept for special purposes, when we really need to use the light, and anyway it is very difficult and time consuming to make the powders in the first place.'

Kel looked a little disappointed at this rebuff, but saw the reasoning behind it, and then cheered up considerably when he was offered another of the sweet tasting shiny black spheres.

'Oh, I meant to have told you earlier, on my way here I came across what I think might be one of the new creatures which has been proving troublesome to our neighbouring group. It was in the main branch and had made a hiding hole deep beneath the bark of the walkway.'

Kel then went on to tell how he had tempted the creature to take his bait, and the marking of the danger spot afterwards.

'You did well Kel, but you must take very great care when approaching such creatures, as they are very quick to act, and so far we don't know very much about them, except that they are new to this area of the forest.

'I've heard from several of the other groups dotted about the forest that they have been experiencing an influx of these new creatures for some time now, and lost quite a few group members, but this is the first time that one of them has come into our area of the forest. I don't know if this is a new breed of animal or one that has migrated into this area, but it is a serious threat none the less, and we must find a way of combating it.' Mec looked pensive as he left the little room and went out into the main cave.

Kel followed, hoping that this wasn't the end of the story telling as he had been looking forward to it for some time.

'I have an idea, but it's only an idea at this stage. You probably don't know about it, but up in the higher layers of the forest there is a plant which produces a large round skin like bag of dust which is deadly to most creatures which inhale it. I have only been told about it as something to avoid at all costs. It would seem that the dust is something like the spores which come from some of the fungi we use, but of a totally different kind to ours, and for some reason it kills just about anything which it contacts.

'We may be able to use it to our advantage if we can find a safe way to handle it and get the creature to take a bite. Anyway, I'll let you know if I come up with some means of ridding us of the creature as I am sure you would want to be in on the kill, as it were.'

Kel sensed that was the end of that particular subject, at least until Mec had worked out how to tackle the creature in more detail.

Mec began to gather up the little pots which lay scattered about the floor of the main cave, and Kel joined him in the task, to delay his leaving by being useful.

'Be careful not to get the contents on your hands.' Mec called out as he arranged the pots he had collected on a shelf at the back of the cave.

'They are not as deadly as the powder bag I was telling you about, but some could give you a nasty skin burn.'

When they had finished tidying up the pots, Kel wondered if he would be asked to leave for the day, and must have shown his thoughts on his face, for Mec said with a smile,

'And now for your questions, young Kel. You deserve some reward for visiting me.'

They both retired to the little room where they had eaten earlier, and after Mec produced some more refreshments, sat down on the gourd stools.

'Well, what's the first story you want to hear.' asked Mec, settling his back against the wall of the room and crossing his outstretched legs.

'The story of the greater and lesser knives, please.' replied Kel politely.

'All right. As you know, the greater knives are only given to those who reach a certain age, which you will soon attain, and there is a very good reason for this. The larger knives are not easy to come by, and are only given to those who will look after them and use them very carefully. The lesser knives are more numerous, and so we can afford to give them to anyone who we think is capable of using them sensibly.

'Now, you are about to ask, how do the knives come about? Well, we make them. There is an area deep in the forest known as the killing sands, and it is from there that we get the material for the knives. A very long time ago, according to legend, it was discovered that a glassy black stone found in the killing sands, if hit with another hard stone, would shatter into long shards, and these pieces are the basis of our knives. There are a lot more of the little shards as some are made when we trim the larger ones to shape. The strange thing is that when the black stone breaks, it always does so leaving a very sharp edge.'

Mec paused to bite into one of the large yellow berries he had brought in, spitting out the seeds with great accuracy into a large gourd pot at his feet while he munched the succulent fruit.

'Sorry Kel, do please help yourself, don't wait for me to ask you. Now where was I?   Oh yes, the knives. The handles which protect your hands from the very sharp cutting edge are also made by us, and without them, the black cutting stones would be of little value to us.'

'We use the juice from the stave plant mixed with fine wood dust scraped from a piece of dead wood. The handle end of the blade is dipped into the mixture and then given a quick dip into a bowl of urine when this has set a little, it is recoated with the juice and wood dust mix, dipped into the urine bowl again, and so on, slowly building up in thickness to form a protective handle.

'So that's how the knives are made. I'm sure you can see why we look after them so very carefully, for not only are they difficult to make, but the getting of the shiny black stones in the first place is not without its difficulties. As I said earlier, those who actually collect the stones from the killing sands die, and do so in a very unpleasant way. Also the sands are a very long way from here, and take several cycles of the greater sun to reach, and just as many for the return journey.

'Usually, those who have been brave enough to recover the shiny stones have died before they can return home. Shortly after leaving the sands, they get very sick, and quite unable to hold any food down for more than a few moments, and then all their body hair loosens and comes out as soon as it is touched by anything. This is followed by black marks like bruises appearing, and shortly after that they die.

'But that was a very, very long time ago. What happens now, and has done for some considerable time, is that when a member of the tribe gets to be very old and near to death, they are taken to the killing sands and there retrieve some of the shiny stones. As they are going to die soon, it is considered the last helpful act that they can do for the group.

'There is no compulsion to do this, but very few refuse. As far as I know, none of the stone gatherers have ever survived long enough to get back to their group area, but as they were so near death anyway, it matters little.'

Kel saw the sad look on Mec's face, and didn't really know what to say, although he felt he should say something.

'The killing sands are linked to several other stories.' Mec said, after a long pause.

'There is one story, or I should say legend, about the giants who walked this world long, long before we were here. They were four or five times as tall as we are, if you can believe that, and lived in 'Sitys', whatever they might be.

'They may be like my tree cave, but a lot larger, I don't know, and I don't know anyone who does. It is said that they had things in which a lot of them could travel, instead of walking as we do, but I can't imagine what they would be like, and it's only a story.'

'Where have all the giants gone?' asked Kel, eager to keep the stories going.

'Nobody knows. It is said there was a time of the Great Lights, very bright lights, much brighter than the greater sun when seen from the top of the forest, and after that there were no more giants, or anything else much for that matter.

'Some story tellers think that the killing sands are something to do with the disappearing giants, but no one knows for sure as it all happened so very long ago, and we have nothing much to go on except the stories themselves.'

'What are the sands like?' asked Kel, his appetite now well and truly whetted for more.

'So it is said, there are several of them throughout the great forest. The one nearest here is like a vast circular area on which nothing will grow, and it would take several cycles of the greater sun to walk across it, although no one has ever done so to my knowledge. It's just fine sand, the like of which you will sometimes find lodged in the base of some of the water gathering plants, blown there by the wind, I would suspect.'

'Sometimes on the surface, and sometimes half buried in the sand, are the shiny black stones. They are very heavy, and like nothing else we have ever found, and not at all like the hard stones we collect from the forest floor.'

Kel noticed that Mec's voice had dropped a tone, and this was usually a signal that the meeting was coming to an end, and he still had a whole host of other questions he wanted to ask. So he didn't take the hint.

'I think it's time you went back to your group, Kel. They will worry about you as the greater sun will soon be giving little light to guide you, and the lesser sun is not due with any brightness for several cycles yet.' Mec clearly saw the look of disappointment on Kel's face and added, 'You can come again tomorrow, and we will discuss how to get rid of the new creature you found today.'

With that, Kel reluctantly got up from his seat, thanked Mec for his time and the stories he had related, and left the tree cave. The light was already beginning to fail, and the weak lesser sun would not be up for a while, so he had to tread carefully along the trail in the middle of the branch, although the branch itself was ten times his height in width.

There was one nasty little creature which made them keep to the well worn pathways, and that was a worm-like thing which would very quickly bore into your foot if you stood too long in any one place. It was very difficult to remove once having gained entry, usually leaving the head imbedded deep in the flesh, and this would then later erupt into a running sore which refused to heal.

For some reason the worm creature didn't like hiding underneath an area which was well trodden, and so Kel and his people kept to the tracks, and the worm stayed in the undisturbed area to the side of the pathways, to catch other unwary prey which didn't know about its hiding place.

Carefully skirting the red marked danger area of the creature he had baited earlier, Kel realized he needed a drink of water, and went up a side branch to where he knew some of the many types of water plants grew.

Although one of the smaller members of the species, the green and yellow striped plant was twice as tall as he was, being composed of a series of sheath like leaves arranged in a circle, water having collected at the base from the frequent rains which dribbled down from the lofty forest canopy above.

Breaking off a thin twig a little longer than his arm, Kel placed one foot on a new bud which was growing out from the base of the plant and reached up to dangle the twig over the lip of the lowest of the cup-shaped water reservoirs. He didn't have long to wait. There was a violent commotion in the water and he withdrew the twig to find a Snapper had a firm grip on the other end of it.

An over sized head equipped with a double row of pure white teeth had a firm grip on the twig and was furiously trying to free itself from what it suddenly realized wasn't a meal after all, but the teeth had penetrated the wood and wouldn't come loose.

Kel deftly flicked the stick with the Snapper attached to it over the side of the cupped shaped leaf, and then tossed it out over the edge of the branch he was standing on. Some moments later it would reach the forest floor and no doubt provide a meal for some hungry denizen of the depths, although there wasn't a lot of flesh on a Snapper as it was all head, and even that was mostly composed of chisel sharp teeth.

Just about every water plant had a Snapper in each compartment, and unless one wanted to lose a large part of one's nose, it was sensible to rid the pool of its occupant before drinking.

He never could understand how the Snapper thing worked. You could rid a pool of its Snapper, and the next time you visited the same pool there would be another one in residence. Never two, just the one. Where did they come from? And always the same size, just big enough to do one a bit of serious damage, but not life threatening.

The forest certainly didn't make life easy for the group, and he supposed all the other creatures felt the same way about it, for everything was chased or eaten by something.

Having freed the pool of its guardian, Kel broke off another twig, and repeated the procedure just in case there was another one present, which there never was, but it was better to be safe than sorry. As the twig didn't try to wrench itself out of his hand, he assumed the pool was now empty of flying teeth, and it was now safe to take a drink.

Gripping the edge of the giant leaf, he heaved himself up to its edge and leaned over to slake his thirst in the cool sweet water. Some of the water plants were true giants, and he and his group had often bathed in them on hot and sticky days, just to get cool again.

By the time that Kel had made his way back to the group, it was getting quite dark, and he had to take extra care on the last leg of his journey crossing from one tree system to the next, as some of the linking branches were quite thin.

Some of the younger ones had already settled down for the night, and finding anyone wide awake and interested enough to hear of his exploits was just as difficult as ever.

He still couldn't understand why such a cavalier attitude was adopted by the other members of his group to any dangers or things of interest he mentioned, it was almost as if they didn't care, and yet their survival depended upon the latest information of any new threats being relayed to them as quickly as possible.

In the end Kel gave up, and he too found a snug spot to sleep through the night, but not before putting his little collection of tinkle stones around the area, hanging them from nearby branches so that if anything should creep up on him while he slept, the stones would be disturbed and hopefully wake him up. Funny, he had shown the others how it worked, but he remained the only one in the whole group to use them.

Food down in the lower levels must have been getting a bit scarce, for during the night something large and well muscled with large saucer like eyes crept up to the group, and with one swift blow from a powerful fore paw, crushed the head of one of the group, flat. A slight whimper was the only sound, followed by the soft rustle of the retreating beast with its meal.

The time during which the lesser sun didn't shine through at this level was their most vulnerable, as creatures which couldn't stand the light found it quite acceptable to come up to see what there was to eat, and yet they took no precautions. Kel couldn't understand that either.

Next morning, as the greater sun broke through the heavy canopy above, there was only a blood stained smear to show what had happened in the darkness of the night, and that was fading fast as a variety of small insects hungrily devoured the food bonanza.

The trail led to one of the main trunks, and a few smudges and scratch marks on the bark showed where the creature had slithered down to the depths below.

When Kel pointed out what had happened, no one except the nearest relatives of the missing group member seemed overly perturbed, and the incident was soon forgotten as the early morning food gathering party set out to find the first meal of the day.

Kel felt he was different to the others of his group, and found it difficult to come to terms with that difference. He really cared what happened to all of them, while they just went through the rote of taking precautions against the perils of the forest. This was something he must mention to the Story Teller, as he may well have an answer for the dissimilarity he felt, and an explanation for the others apparent indifference to the dangers around them.

A small party of them were asked to harvest some more staves for the group, and Kel went along to help as he quite enjoyed stave gathering. They trooped out of the main area where the females and younger ones usually stayed until midday, and made their way across several main junctions of the larger branches to where an old tree had at last succumbed to the ravages of time, and crumpled to the forest floor deep below them, leaving a brightly lit area in which the stave plants thrived in great abundance.

The party had split up into threes and fours, working on their own chosen clumps, and Kel, the youngest of his group, took over as team leader. No one seemed to mind, and they took their orders from him without question, cutting the poles from the main plant as he indicated his choice. He once wondered what would happen if he suddenly said 'Jump off this branch,' and wouldn't have been too surprised if they had done so.

Kel was just about to say that they had collected enough staves, when a yell from the party next to him cut through the air, causing a flurry of various flying creatures to take flight and several other oddities to scurry for cover.

One of the group had turned around too quickly and hit one of his fellows in the chest with the sap dripping end of a stave. The unfortunate was clutching his chest, trying to remove the sticky juice and getting it on his fingers.

'Lay down quickly.' yelled Kel, but the sheer terror of the situation had paralysed the recipient of the sticky deadly juice, and he just stood there yelling. Kel took a couple of quick steps forward and kicked the unfortunate's legs out from under him, sending the body crashing down onto the track.

'You two, wet his chest, quickly!' yelled Kel with a voice of authority.'

'But that will ...'

'Do it, now!' he almost screamed back at the hesitant onlookers.

Unfortunately, most of them had emptied their bladders either at early morning ablutions, or while treating the ends of the staves they had cut, so it was some moments before anyone was found with enough of the necessary fluid and the ability to release it.

Eventually one of the group managed to produce a rather pathetic dribble, and then two members of another team who had been working on the fringe of the stave clumps came forward with a plentiful supply.

Grabbing a bunch of leaves, Kel managed to remove most of the sticky white juice from the left hand of the man now writhing on the track, while the two standing over him did their best to direct a wavering stream of steaming urine onto his chest. Kel wetted the man's hand and then told one of the onlookers to continue to keep it wet, while he inspected the rest of the body for signs of the juice.

Luckily, it was only the chest and one hand which were contaminated, and Kel waited patiently for the juice on the man's chest to congeal enough to pull it free without getting stuck to it himself. It had already turned a dark amber colour, and the groans of the man on the track were turning to cries of anger as the enthusiastic couple spraying his chest took their eyes off the target to see what Kel was doing, and were in effect giving him a general bath.

'All right, that's enough,' Kel said, 'it should be hard enough now.' The two sprayers moved back, while Kel removed his lesser cutting knife from its pouch and bent over the man on the trackway who was now being held down by the arms and legs following Kel's shouted instructions.

'All of you gather around, watch, listen and remember what I'm about to do,' Kel said with a ring of authority in his voice, 'it's important that you remember this, and tell all the others who go out to gather staves.' There was dead silence, and all eyes were on him as if he had just made the greatest pronouncement of all time.

'I'm going to cut the lump of congealed juice free from the hair on his chest and then try to pull it off. At worst, he will have a bald patch where the juice has reached the skin and stuck, and a very sore chest for a few days, but at least he won't be dead.'

With that, Kel began to cut the hair surrounding the now hardened juice, and eventually managed to prise up one corner so that he could get a firm grip on it.

'This is going to hurt a little, perhaps a lot, but you will still live and it will heal in time.'

For the recumbent figure on the trackway seeing the lesser cutting knife, Kel with a determined look on his face and the thought of immediate surgery on his chest, it was too much, and renewed his yelling.

'Hold him down tightly.' Kel shouted, trying to make himself heard above the din, and a pile of bodies descended on the prospective patient, pinning him flat to the path.

Kel took a firm grip on the patch of hardened resin, and with one swift jerk ripped it free of the man's chest, taking with it a goodly portion of skin and the attached hair.

The ensuing scream rent the otherwise quiet forest air, sending the remainder of the local creatures scurrying for cover at a speed they weren't used to, several missing their footing and subsequently dropping to the depths below.

The patient had now passed out, and was lying still and peaceful on the branch, a red patch of raw skin oozing blood and trickling down the side of his chest. Kel went over to one of the side branches and rummaged about for a while, returning with a bunch of a soft moss like growth, and thrust it between the top of the patient's legs.

'Wet this.' he said to the whimpering creature on the trackway, who had now regained some degree of consciousness, but his bladder had emptied when the patch of solidified resin had been pulled off, and it didn't look as if there was any left.

The patient finally found the strength to sit up and begin complaining, he wanted to wash off the copious amounts of urine contributed so generously by his companions. The stave collecting party broke up, most carrying the harvested staves back to the main group, while three joined Kel and his irate patient, who set off looking for a large water plant.

Apart from the odd complaint from the one with the sore chest, the group plodded on in relative silence, the slap slap of their feet on the smooth bark of the pathway being the only sound.   Kel wondered how long it would be before the whole incident would be forgotten, and little, if anything, learnt from the experience.

A sharp plop broke the otherwise stillness of the forest, as a large yellow wobbly fruit fell from above, and burst open just ahead of the little band of travellers. With one accord all heads looked up to find the source of the gift, for the wobbly fruit was not abundant in this part of the forest, and was greatly prized by all.

The vine from which the fruit had dropped was suspended from a branch high up in the canopy, and well out of their reach. Normally, only fruit actually picked from the vine was eaten, as when it had matured enough to fall of its own accord, it had fermented to the degree that two of them would put the average consumer into a state of euphoria, and reduce leg stability to a level that was down right dangerous, hence its name.

There was no way they could reach the suspended fruits without a tedious climb up into the higher canopy, but a few of the over ripe fruits had fallen onto patches of thick moss which was growing on the side of the trackway, and these hadn't burst open.

The temptation was too much for them, and all hurried forward, eager to secure a helping of one of the most pleasant flavours provided by nature.

'Only one fruit each.' Kel called out, knowing full well he was wasting his breath, but felt he should make the effort anyway.

The patient had consumed four of the delicious yellow fruits, and had ceased to complain about his chest as the joyous little band helped to support him on their way to the nearest large water plant.

By the time they had located a plant big enough to dunk their companion in, the fruit had taken full effect, and Kel had great difficulty in preventing the other three from heaving the patient straight into the huge bowl like pool of water without first fishing out the snapper.

'Oh come on,' cried Kel, 'remember the drill for water plants. You must remove the Snapper before you drink, let alone dump our friend in the pool.' The other three abandoned their attempts to launch their companion into the pool, and stood giggling.

Eventually a twig was found, dipped into the pool and the Snapper extracted from its watery home. The one who had the Snapper on the end of the twig waved it in front of his companion, who promptly ran off, the twig waver following close behind.

'Come back you fools.' yelled Kel.

At which point the snapper had somehow wriggled off the end of the twig and was now somewhere on the trackway.

Both the chased and chaser returned to the water plant a lot faster than they had left it, and looked suitably frightened, glancing around them wondering where the snapper had got to. After a stern ticking off from Kel for their dangerous behaviour, they checked the pool again for Snappers, and then helped the patient, who by this time was on the point of going to sleep, into the pool.

The sudden submergence in the cool water of the plant pool

returned the patient to a sufficient degree of consciousness to begin complaining again. Kel finally lost his patience with the whole affair, slashing the base of the plant pool with his lesser knife.

The giant leaf split open at the base, and the contents roared out in a raging torrent, nearly washing the four bystanders off their feet. As the water pressure dropped, the patient shot out of the now enlarged split in the leaf, and if Kel hadn't been so quick in grabbing him, he too would have joined the huge volume of water which was now cascading down in a shattered silver stream to the forest floor below.

This turn of events tended to sober them up a little, and it was a more circumspect little party who eventually returned to the main group, the patient now adorned with a patch of urine soaked soggy moss strapped to his chest, and with the promise from Kel that it would heal up in time after a visit to Mec for medication.

Two:
The Quest

Remembering the Story Teller's invitation to visit him again, Kel partook of the midday break for food, and then left the main group to their own devices. He was as bored with them as they must have felt at his constant chiding and suggestions for a better and safer life in the forest.

The red marker was still in place as he passed the point where he had baited the creature beneath the trackway yesterday, and he felt tempted to try and bait it again for something amusing to do, but then thought the Story Teller's tales would be far more interesting, and left them it to wait for something or someone else to come along.

Mec welcomed him like an old friend, and they were soon deep in conversation about the morning's events.

'It was bright of you to suggest using urine soaked moss for that poor man's chest, where did you get the idea from?'

'I don't know,' replied Kel, 'it just seemed the right thing to do at the time, somehow.'

'That's interesting. It is the right thing to do in circumstances like that. But the most interesting thing is the reason behind it. Urine is pure, and contains no fungus spores or anything else which might harm you, so if you have a cut, it is the best thing to wash it clean with.

'There are many things like this which would benefit you to know, and if you are willing, I will relate them to you.'

The usual fruit selection was passed to Kel, and they both ate in silence for a while, Kel having the feeling that Mec had something on his mind, and would no doubt come out with it when he was good and ready.

'I have often thought of late,' said Mec at long last, 'that you're not happy staying within your group, just stumbling on from day to day. You find it boring, unfulfilling. Am I right?'

'Well, yes,' said Kel, 'I haven't given it much thought, I must admit, but come to think about it, you are absolutely right. I am fed up of trying to tell them how to improve their lives, but they just don't seem interested. They don't seem to mind if they do stupid things which could endanger them. I don't understand it at all, can you explain it for me?'

'Well yes and no.' Mec wasn't being awkward, he just didn't know how much to tell Kel, and how much he would understand.

'I think I shall have to tell you some more of the old stories, and see how much of them you understand. From that I shall be able to judge how much to tell you of what I know, and have heard. There is a big difference between legend and the stories I have, and somewhere in the middle they merge, so one is never too sure what is true and what is just an old folk tale which has been passed on down through the ages, and no doubt altered on the way.'

'Would you rather I asked the questions I have in mind?' asked Kel, somehow knowing Mec wouldn't.

'No, I think I'll stick to doing what I know I do best, and we'll see how we go from there.

'The first story is about the trees. According to the old legends, the trees were not always as tall as they are now. Back in the old days of the giants, that's if they really existed at all, the trees were said to be only as tall as ten to fifteen giants standing on each others heads, and were usually no bigger around than about six giants holding hands around their girth.

'Each tree stood on its own piece of ground, although the branches of one tree may have touched the next, they didn't join together as they do now.   Each tree was a separate thing on its own, and this is maybe the reason why they didn't grow so tall, as the wind would have blown them down.'

'You could liken it to a small group of people. If they were all standing together without touching each other, it would be easy to push any one of them down, but if they were all holding on to each other and you tried to push one over, you couldn't do it because the others would support that person. It's the same way with the trees we now have, but, according to legend, it wasn't always so.

'Now, as soon as a branch touches another branch or main trunk, they join up. In effect, this means that the forest is really one huge tree with lots of main trunks going down to the ground beneath. This gives it tremendous strength, and as they need the light of the greater sun, they keep on growing up to reach it.

'Another interesting thing, the giants are supposed to have cut down certain trees, and then cut them up to make things, I don't understand that myself. But then, there are many things about them I don't understand!'

'We cut the stave plants to make our staves from, so maybe it was something similar with the giants.' said Kel.

Mec hid his little grin, this young man was catching on fast. Maybe he was right in his choice, after all.

'The next story also concerns the giants. They are supposed to have made things, as you do, like the staves, but these things the giants made were huge, and powerful by all accounts. It is said that the things which they made led to their downfall in the end.

'They are supposed to have flown in the air like some of the flying lizards and the huge birds which live in the top of the forest, but I don't see how that's possible. And another strange tale, it is also said that they could float on water, and went great distances on it, but we know that water pools are only quite small really, and can be walked around without much trouble.'

'As you know, you are limited to making simple things, like gourd cups and bowls, and the staves. Perhaps the taboo against making things comes from the time of the giants. If we make powerful things, maybe we would go the way of the giants.'

'I don't see why.' retorted Kel, suspecting that Mec was going to turn out to be just like the others in the group, no interest in anything new.

'I don't see why we shouldn't make anything which will help us to survive better. There's always something new threatening us. This new creature under the trackway bark is a good example. If we don't find a way of getting rid of it, we will be confined to little areas of the forest where it doesn't want to go, and if enough of them turn up, that'll leave us no room at all.' Kel was getting a little cross, and didn't bother to hide it.

'But what about the taboo which discourages us from making things?' asked Mec.

'To my way of thinking, that's a load of old superstition, and not really worthy of real consideration.' replied Kel, really warming up to the argument.

'It isn't the things we make which could cause so much trouble, but the people who use them. A stave is just a piece of wood, and a Cutting Knife is just a piece of special stone with a sharp edge, it's what we do with them that really counts. Perhaps the giants had something like the Wobbly fruit, or something which gave the same effect, and things got out of control.'

Mec was very pleased that Kel took up the argument, and gave as good as he got. He hadn't been wrong in his estimation of the young lad. Mec decided that now was the right time to tell Kel what he really had in mind all along, and then proceeded to do so.

'As you may know, we Story Tellers keep in touch with each other, exchanging ideas and knowledge. We are the keepers of the Stories, making sure that they are passed on down through the generations, and kept as pure as possible.

'As well as dispensing medical herbs to the sick, setting broken bones and trying to enlighten the groups for which we are responsible, it is our duty, or so we feel, to pick out bright young people like yourself, and try to get them to expand the frontiers of our knowledge by exploring the forest and what ever may lie beyond.

'I have chosen you to be my explorer, to go forth and see what is really out there which we don't know about, and hopefully bring back that knowledge for the good of all.

'There is another group like ours, not too far from here, and it has a bright young lad like you who doesn't like his life as it is. I have arranged for him to visit us after the midday food break, so he should be here soon. I would like you to be friends with him, and see if you think he would make a good companion for you in the future. I can't see you staying with the group much longer, and the only other thing to do is explore the forest, and for that you will need someone to help you and share in the discoveries you may come across.'

Kel looked surprised, things were moving along a lot faster than he had expected, and the concept of leaving the group for an extended period of time had not occurred to him before. The idea of a companion was a good one, and he felt the better for it.

'There is one more tale I would like to tell you a little more about. It is to do with the time of the Great Lights. We don't know what they were or who brought them about, but we think it was something to do with the things which the giants had made, and probably got out of their control.'

'The stories are very old, and most likely have been altered as they have come down through the ages, but the main thing is, we think they are connected with the Death Sands.

'We know of several of these areas of sand throughout the forest, and you must keep well away from them. It is all right to view them from the trees, but not from the trees which have changed around the edges of the sands and are unlike the trees we have around us now.

'Any area you come across in which nothing is growing must be avoided at all costs, as it may have the same properties as the Death Sands. We don't know this for sure, but it is better to be safe than sorry afterwards, and the 'afterwards' is not very long according to the tales

I have heard. No doubt you will come across many strange plants and creatures, and you must, at all costs, treat them as if they are deadly to you, until you can be sure they aren't, by whatever means you have at your disposal.'

Suddenly the Story Teller raised his head, listening intently, but Kel hadn't heard a thing.

'I think our visitor is approaching,' said Mec, tilting his head 'I can hear faint footsteps outside on the main branch.'

A few moments later a young sounding voice called out,

'Mec, are you there?'

'Yes, come in Moss and meet my friend Kel.'

A tall well muscled youth of about the same age as Kel strode purposefully into the main cave and over to the entrance of the little den in which Mec and Kel were sitting on their gourd stools.

'I'd like you to meet Moss, he's from a nearby group, and like you, he is not too happy with his lot in life. He thinks there must be more to it than just existing and plodding on from day to day, and so I have brought you both together to see if you would like to go on an adventure.'

Kel stood up and took a few steps over towards the youth as he entered the room, and touched palms, as was the traditional form of greeting between strangers. He was a little taller than Kel, with broader shoulders and a deeper bronze coloured body hair, but apart from that, they could have been brothers.

'I understand you are as bored with life here in the forest as I am.' said Kel, not knowing what else to say.

'I didn't used to be,' replied the youth 'until Mec here began telling me the stories, and then I wanted to go out and see for myself what truth there was in them.'

Mec had brought out another bowl of fruits and pods, and they both tucked in to a good feed, almost as if they were subconsciously trying to put off the next stage of events which would irrevocably join them together in the adventure Mec intended them to go on.

At last appetites were fully satiated, and the three of them sat back with bloated stomachs, looking at one another, wondering who would start the conversation of no return.

'You are both coming up to the age when you will be presented with the Greater Cutting Knives, but I have something here which will make that seem a small event.' and so saying, Mec went into another of the little rooms, returning with two of the biggest knives they had ever seen, complete with two scabbards and the holding belts.

'These are rather special knives, and were made a long time ago by a friend of mine. I somehow knew this day would come, and I wanted my adventurers to be equipped with the best I could find, and these are the best.'

Each of the shimmering black knives were nearly as long as Kel's fully extended arm, and had a slight curve to the blades which made them look even more deadly than the normal straight type.

The handle was moulded so that it fitted the three fingers and prehensile thumb of the holder and was adorned with a bright red stone on the extreme end, and a strap through which the holder's hand could be passed so that the knife wouldn't be dropped if it was let go for any reason. Mec next produced the scabbards to hold the knives, which had a series of little pockets on one side, each containing a smaller knife than the one before, the final one being only as long as Kel's little finger.

'These represent a complete workshop, as it were. There is a knife for every purpose, and they are made out of the hardest of the Shiny Black Stones we have ever found, and if looked after, should last you a full lifetime.'

The pair were overwhelmed at the sight of the knives, having never seen any so large and magnificently made. Mec slid the gleaming black blade back into its scabbard, almost with an air of reverence, and handed each of them a belted scabbard with its complete set of knives.

'There is one more thing about these knives. You will notice there is a bright red stone set in the handle.

'These stones were found together a long time ago, and are set in the end of a hard silver coloured tube. We had no idea what they are for or who made them, but we think it must be a leftover from the time of the giants.

'They have been passed down through generations of Story Tellers, and recently we found out by accident that if you pressed the stone hard enough, the other stone emitted a 'pinging' sound. It's almost as if they talk to each other, and distance seems to make little difference.

'Up until recently we didn't have a use for these stones, but now it was thought a good idea to set them into the end of the Knife handles, so that if one of you ever needed help, he could summon the other.'

'Let me show you how it works.' and Mec handed Kel one of the scabbards, giving the other one to Moss.

'Go into the other room, no, go outside onto the main branch and walk along it some way, when you hear the 'ping', press the stone on your scabbard, and then return.'

Moss disappeared out of the cave entrance, and after a few moments Mec indicated to Kel it was time to press the stone, which he did. Almost instantly there was a loud 'ping' from Kel's scabbard, and he nearly dropped it in surprise, and was still looking in amazement at the device when Moss returned to the room with a grin on his face.

'That's the nearest thing to magic I've ever experienced.' said Moss, hanging on to the scabbard as if his life depended upon it.

'Is it now.' Mec rejoined with a grin, 'wait until you see the next item I have for you.' He hurried away to return with a small gourd bowl containing a little water and a small black stick with a white mark on one end.

'If anything is magic, then this is.' said Mec as he place the bowl on the floor of the room. Rummaging about on a shelf, he produced a small piece of bark and placed it on the water in the bowl, and then put the black stick on top of the floating piece of bark.

Before their eyes, the piece of bark together with the black stick, slowly rotated on the water, eventually coming to rest pointing towards the doorway.

'Now that's what I call magic.' said Mec, sitting back on his stool and waiting to see what reaction it produced from the two youths.

'What makes it turn?' asked Kel, giving it a poke with his finger and watching in fascination as the little black stick on it's piece of bark gyrated round, to slowly come to rest pointing in the same position as before.

'We don't know,' replied Mec, 'but wherever you take it, and how ever much you spin it around, it always points in the same direction, and that's towards the Greater Sun at about the time of the midday meal.'

It was Moss's turn to twirl the black stick around, which he did several times.

'This is another piece of equipment I think you should take with you on your expedition, the reason being if you just wander about in the forest, you could well go around in circles, and not know it. With this device, you can check that you are going in a chosen direction, and more or less in a straight line. Let me show you.'

Mec arose from his seat and picked up the little bowl.

'If I wanted to go towards that room over there, all I have to do is make a little mark on the side of the bowl,' which he did, 'And then make sure that the stick points towards it. If I go off to one side, the stick will no longer point in the direction of the mark, so I just turn until it does line up, and walk on, and here I am in the other room.' said Mec, his voice fading as he disappeared into the small room opposite.

'This is the only piece of the black pointing stick we have ever found, so look after it very carefully.

Kel wondered what other magical things Mec might have hidden away in his caves, but didn't like to ask. And then a bright idea formed in his mind which he hesitated to mention for a moment, but then the excitement of it overcame his reluctance and he blurted it out.

'You know that clear body shell you used for the light maker? 'Well, if we could get another one, and cut it to fit the top of the pointing bowl and then seal it together with juice from the stave plant, the water would not run out if it got tipped over.'

'And we wouldn't have to worry about carrying water to keep filling the bowl up, and we could still see the pointing stick.' It all came out in one long burst, and Kel was a little out of breath as he finished.

'Now that's good thinking,' said Mec, 'I've got some old insect cases somewhere, and you can have a go tomorrow and see what you come up with. Now, before you two can go off on your exploration, there's one job I'd like you to do, and that's get rid of the new creature which you found hiding under the bark on the main branch not far from here.

'It will be good experience for you both, working out how you will do it, and then you must try to get others of your respective groups skilled in the matter, or at least interested in the method of disposing of the creatures.'

'You said you knew of a 'Dust Ball' or something like that, which was poisonous to just about everything, where can we find it?' asked Kel.

'I know where to find them, but it isn't easy and will involve a journey up into the next level of the forest.

'The bag-like structure is easily broken when they are ripe, and they would have to be ripe to be effective, so you will have to work out some means of transferring them down here without endangering yourselves.' Mec wasn't going to make it easy for the two.

'May we come here tomorrow and discuss it with you' asked Kel, a little worried that his taller and slightly larger companion might take the initiative and come up with an answer to the problem before he could.

'Yes, you may, but make it as early as possible in the morning as there will be a lot to do if we are going to go up to the next level, and I would like each of you to bring one other from your group so that they may learn from what we are about to do.'

'Make sure it is the brightest member of your group, for they will have to learn how to rid the area of these new creatures after you leave.' said Mec, nodding and lowering his head, the customary sign that the meeting was coming to an end.

Kel and Moss got up to leave, clutching the newly acquired knife scabbards tightly to them, but Mec held out his hands with a smile and said, 'You have to earn these first, and they certainly can't be shown to the groups, it would cause too many enquiries as to where they came from.'

When the two were outside the cave again and about to go their separate ways, Moss turned back towards Kel and said,

'I can see his point, but those knives are ours, one way or another. See you in the morning, Kel.   Oh, and I'm very pleased to have met you.   Between us, we should be able to sort out that creature, whatever it is.' and with that he was gone, a fleeting shadow among the other shadows, dancing along a main branch and then flickering out of sight.

Kel returned to his group, carefully going around the marked area on the main branch homewards where the creature lay hidden, and wondering just how they were going to deal with this new threat to their survival.

The man who had lost some of his chest hair in the stave collecting escapade was still wittering on about his misfortune and looking generally miserable. Kel examined the wound which was already beginning to heal over, and told him to keep the moss damp.

There was no sign of the dreaded fungus infection and Kel tried to cheer him up by saying a full recovery was most likely, but it made little difference to his general demeanour, and Kel began to lose patience, telling him he was lucky to be alive. All he got for his trouble was a long face and a parting scowl as he left.

They all settled down for the night, Kel setting up his ring of 'Tinkle stones' as usual, and wondering why no one else had ever asked him why he did it, or even what they were for. Yes, he would be glad to leave this dumb bunch of idiots. The more he thought about it, the more he warmed towards his new companion, Moss. He at least had a spark of life in him, and could no doubt be relied upon in a crisis, and there were likely to be quite a few of them.

It had rained hard in the night, and they were all wet and looking fed up next morning, except Kel who had the foresight to curl up under an overhanging branch and was warm and dry when he went out to look for his first meal of the new day.

The Greater Sun had only just broken through the higher levels and spilled a little dim light onto Kel's group when he set about selecting one of their number to join him on the creature clearing exercise. No one seemed very interested in the project, although he had explained it in detail and told them what would most likely happen if they did nothing. In the end, one of the older members said he would join Kel, but if this was for the greater good of the group or just to appease Kel, he had no idea.

The pair set off armed with their staves, and Kel pointed out the danger area as they approached it. The older man didn't seem to be the least perturbed at the possibility of being devoured by the hidden creature, and Kel wondered if he was just wasting his time.

When they finally reached Mec's tree cave, Moss and his chosen companion were already there, and while they exchanged greetings between them in the traditional manner, Kel couldn't help but notice that Moss was certainly a lot more lively and brighter than the member of his group he had chosen to bring along.

Mec came out to greet them all and explained in great detail the possible dangers of the expedition, and the need to clear the forest in their area of the new threat. Five new staves were produced from the tree cave, and Mec explained that these were a little different in that they had a small Lesser Cutting Knife set in the end, and great care would be needed if no one was to be cut while they climbed up into the higher levels.

'There is a thong attached on the butt end of each stave so that it can be attached to your carrying belt, and the sharp end will then dangle well below you as you climb, but the climber below will have to be aware of getting his head cut open if he isn't careful and doesn't keep his distance from the one above.'

The party set off, climbing up a series of steps cut into the main trunk until the smaller side branches above were reached, augmented by a convenient dangling of vines to give the necessary handholds.

At one point Mec called a halt to the climbing, and they all gathered together in the crotch of a main branch and the massive towering trunk. He had cocked his head on one side, and was listening intently for something.

'Can you hear that faint buzzing sound?' he asked. Moss said he could but the others all shook their heads.

'That is the sound of a nest of Stinger Flies, about the size of your clenched fist, and if they attack us we will all be dead in a few moments. The noise is caused by some of the larger ones at the entrance to their hollowed out home in the trunk, blowing air into it for the others to breathe. So far none have come out this early, so I'll climb up a little to see if I can find their entrance hole. You had better stay down here, and if I am attacked, get down to the lower levels as quick as you can.'

Mec carefully made his way up to the next branch, stopped and craning his head back to get a better view of the main trunk above, decided it was safe to go up a little higher, and moved on up to the next intersection of branches.

'It looks as if he has found something.' said Kel, as the figure above looked intently at a spot on the main trunk, but the watchers below could see little detail of what he was looking at.

Mec took a short tube of wood from his belt, pulled a plug from one end, tapped the other end of the tube on the heal of his hand and then carefully withdrew the other plug.

Next he inflated his lungs as full as he could, inserted the tube into a hole in the trunk and applying his mouth to the other end of the tube, exhaled, his breath whistling out, and audible to the watchers below.

Mec came down to join the others at such a speed they thought he must lose his footing and fall into the depths below, but he was more nimble than they had supposed, and reached them safely, a little out of breath and grinning widely.

'That should give them something to think about,' he managed to say at last.

'It's a powder made by grinding up a certain kind of dried fungi, it seems to put them to sleep, or at least make them disinterested in coming out to see what's going on. We'll give it a few moments to be sure it has worked and then we can go on up.

'Fortunately for us, there aren't many of these nests around here as they are a much sought after food for something else even nastier, and I hope we don't meet any of them.'

At last Mec got his breath back and the others had stopped shaking, so the party moved laboriously on up into the canopy above.

'Why didn't you just stop up the hole of those flying things to keep them in?' asked Kel.

'They have more than one hole to their nests, otherwise the air wouldn't flow through. The other one might be some distance away, and they move very quickly.' replied Mec.

'Is that what you're looking for?' Moss was pointing at a dark brown, almost black, bag like thing, dangling on the end of a vine just ahead of them.

'Yes, that's one, and it looks quite ripe.' answered Mec,

'Now what do you propose we do?'

Moss and Kel got into deep discussion on methods of removing the Bag from its vine and carrying it back to their area of the forest, but didn't like the idea of actually handling the deadly looking thing.

The final solution to their problem came from Moss, who suggested that they attach another vine at the top of the Bag, cut the hanging vine free and then they could each hold one of the vines, the bag of spores hanging some distance between them.

It was Moss, who without being asked, ran along the main branch tapping with his stave as he went to disclose anything hidden under the bark, finally arriving at the main point where the vine was attached to the tree branch. Reaching down with one arm he managed to get a grip on it, and bit by bit, eased it up onto the top surface of the trackway, wrapping it around a plant stem to hold it secure.

'Kel, while I haul the Bag up, can you get another vine and tie it on where this vine joins the top of the Bag?'

'On my way,' Kel called back, eager to be doing something towards the project. He ran along the branch to a junction where a group of vines had sprouted from a mass of collected dead foliage and draped themselves over the main branch to hang down into the darkening depths below.

After Kel had selected a suitable vine, he severed it with his lesser knife and was nearly pulled off the branch, fighting hard to regain his balance before letting the vine go slithering and crashing down to the forest floor below.

'There must have been something on the other end of that one.' called Mec. In the same instant a scream rent the otherwise still air, fading as its originator sped ever downwards.

'Everyone lay flat, and dead still.' yelled Mec as the soft whoop whoop of leather covered wings grew closer. A dark shadow glided overhead blotting out the light of the Greater Sun for a moment, and then was gone.

'That was a close one.' said Mec, relief sounding in his voice, 'It must have been nearby and was attracted by the dying wail of whatever was on the end of your vine.'

'What was that?' asked Kel.

'It's a bit like an elongated Snapper Bag, but very much bigger, and with more teeth. They usually live in the upper reaches of the forest where there is more room for them to fly about, but when they get old, they sometimes come down here where there is less competition for their food. They are attracted by motion and noise, so if you keep dead still, they will usually pass you by. We don't see them very often, which is just as well as one of us would only make a light meal for one of them.'

While Moss pulled the Bag up and Kel selected another vine, tugging on it first to make sure he didn't get caught out a second time, the supernumeraries from the two groups just stood around, looking as if they had no interest in the goings on at all.

Whether they were learning anything from the operation or not wasn't clear, as they said nothing and didn't do much either, keeping well clear of the operation.

Mec quietly acted as overseer, his eyes never leaving his prodigies except to scan the forest every now and again for intruders to their area.

Kel finally got the vine up from the lower levels and cut out a section of a thickness to match that of the rope-like tendril from which the Bag grew. Moss had hauled the Bag up to the lower level of the main branch, but it was still out of reach as far as attaching Kel's vine to it was concerned.

'Now what?' asked an exasperated Kel, 'I can't reach the Bag, and Moss can't haul it up any further or it will break against the rough bark of the branch.'

'That's for you two to work out.' replied Mec firmly, and they both knew they were on their own with the problem.

'I'll cut another vine, tie it around my waist and then I can lower myself down and tie on the other vine.' Kel suggested.

'Sounds all right to me, I could lower you down though.' replied Moss, who had tied off the tendril from the Bag to the same stump he had used before.

When Kel was almost level with the bag, Moss called out,

'May I suggest that you tie the knot on the Bag vine some way up, and then slip it down and tighten it, that way there is less chance of bursting it.' Mec smiled to himself, yes he had chosen wisely.

With the second vine made fast, Moss helped a rather sweaty Kel back up onto the branch and they both sat down to get their breath back after the struggle.

'If I cut the Bag's vine, leaving it long enough to keep it a safe distance from us later, and you take the load as I do it, we'll have most of the hard work done.' Moss commented, 'I take one vine and you take the other one, and the Bag will swing in the middle, that way we can stop it hitting anything as we move back along the branch and then we can lower it down ahead of us later.'

Mec was watching, ready to stop the two if they made an unwise move.

Slowly they manoeuvred the deadly bag of dusty spores back along the branch to the main trunk, and began the long descent, the Bag suspended on the two vines below them.

'I hope that huge flying thing doesn't come back and grab it after all our hard work.' Kel panted as he transferred the weight of his load over to Moss, and climbed down to take up his new position below. Bit by bit, by passing the heavy weight of the Bag between them and each moving on to a new position, they got it safely back down to the branch outside Mec's cave.

'Now the fun begins.' said Moss as he tied off the vine around a convenient bough to prevent their prize from slipping into the inky darkness below.

The little group stood around wondering what to do next. They had the deadly dust bag, but how were they going to get it into the cavity in the main branch where the creature lived? Kel came to the rescue after considerable thought on the matter.

'If one of us skirts around the marked spot on the branch taking one of the vines and the other holds on to the other vine at this end, we should be able to swing the Bag along under the branch until it's level with the creature's hiding place. Then we'll have to lift the Bag up on it's vines and drop it very carefully onto the marked spot, the creature should detect the presence of it and take it inside, and then we run!'

Mec nodded his head, not so much for their benefit, but as a self acknowledgement that they had got it right.

'I think we'll need our two companions to help with the final lift.' Kel said, 'It'll be quite difficult to lift and lower it gently onto the branch.'

'All right, let's do it.' called Moss, taking one of the vines and going out along the branch towards the place where the creature lay hidden.

The Bag was slowly swung along beneath the main branch, each of the vine holders making sure in turn that it didn't snag on anything below them, until Moss had gone around the creature's lair and was in position to do the lift.

'This is where we need some help.' said Kel, beckoning his helper towards him, but the man held back, fear clearly seen on his face.

'Oh, come on you stupid little man, if you don't learn how to get rid of these things, they'll get us all in the end.' Kel's patience was running out, no doubt affected by his own fear of what might go wrong.

Reluctantly the helper was shamed into joining Kel and took hold of the vine as if it was going to devour him at any moment.

Moss's helper joined him, after sufficient cajoling, and together they pulled the vines apart, the Bag gradually rising until it was level with the top of the branch.

'Gently now.' called Moss, as the container of dust spores swung over the target area.

'Lower it slowly and then tie the vines off onto anything nearby.' Kel called, sweat running down his face and stinging his eyes.

Moss ran back to join the others and they all stood there, expecting the creature to come out to see what had landed on its trap. Nothing happened, and a look of disappointment was evident on all their faces.

'Now what are you going to do?' asked Mec, leaning back on a side branch, seemingly uninterested about the whole affair, but watching with the fatherly care of one who is very much concerned.

'How about one of us taps on the bark with a stave, that should get it interested in seeing what's going on?'

Mec was visibly enjoying the situation, and didn't bother to hide it.

Kel picked up the longest stave and cautiously moved forward. A couple of sharp taps on the bark trapdoor produced the required effect.

The two halves of the trap dropped inwards, a large viciously clawed tentacle swept up and outwards, scooping the bag of spores into its grasp and both disappeared into the cavern beneath the surface, the trapdoor springing back into place, leaving the branch as if nothing had happened.

Before anyone could say anything, there was a muffled thump and the massive branch on which they were all standing trembled, the trapdoor opened outwards and the two halves flew high up into the air followed by a large puff of mist like dust. The main branch trembled several more times as something heavy inside it thrashed about in abject fury and agony.

As the first pulse of dust began to drift away another one followed in quick succession along with some wood fragments as the head of the creature sprang into view. It was larger than any of the onlookers, and a wicked set of flashing white teeth snapped and ground as the hideous thing tried to find out what was causing all the pain.

The little group cowered back, too petrified to move, let alone run, and watched in horror as the dark muddy grey creature extruded itself from the hole in the branch in a cloud of dust spores and shattered bark fragments. The dust drifted away slowly and just below the fearsome head where the long neck broadened out to form the main body, a pair of tentacle like arms protruded, each equipped with a set of razor sharp curved claws.

The creature, fully six times in length compared to any one of them, and twice as thick, curled and writhed on the branch surface, ripping out large chunks of bark as it tried to destroy anything within its reach, finally sliding over the edge to begin its long drop to the forest floor below.

The high pitched scream emitted by the creature caused the group to clap their hands over their ears to try and shut out the hideous sound, as the creature fell writhing in agony, bouncing off the branches below. The sounds grew fainter as the moments passed, and silence eventually returning to the forest glade.

'Well,' said Moss, 'that wasn't too bad, was it?' but there was a slight tremble in his voice.

The Greater Sun's light dimmed slightly as it filtered down through the leafy canopy above, and the little group, still a bit shaken at the turn of events, headed for Mec's tree cave to shelter from the coming storm.

High above them the lightning crackled and spluttered while enormous quantities of rain crashed down on the upper layers of the forest. As the huge drops hit the leaves and branches they broke up into smaller ones, so by the time they had filtered down to Mec's cave, they were no larger than small grapes. This sudden flood washed all the remaining fungus dust from the main branch.

As quickly as the storm had come, it went, and the Greater Sun sent it's bright light down through the foliage to illuminate the soaking wet branches, turning all colours a shade darker as they absorbed the water.

The little party in the tree cave tucked in to a meal of fruits and pods supplied by Mec, and by the time they had finished, the forest had soaked up all the extra moisture, and only a few wisps of rising mist were left to show what had happened.

'Let's go see what the creature's home is like, it should be safe enough now.' said Mec, and they all trooped out and along the now dry main branch towards the hole, now minus its trapdoor. Moss was the first to lean over the gaping cavity in the branch, Kel holding his feet in case he slipped in.

'It's huge, and I can see a tunnel going back along the main branch for quite a distance.'

'It should be safe enough to go down and have a good look around, but be careful.' said Mec, passing a length of vine to the others around the hole. One end was fastened to a nearby side branch, and Moss and Kel slid down into the hole, with knife tipped staves at the ready.

The two disappeared for a few moments, and then called up to the others on the rim of the hole.

'It looks as if there is a natural hole running back along the branch for as far as we can see, and the creature has left teeth marks where it has enlarged some sections in order to get this far. The main chamber has been cut out and enlarged by the look of it, as there are teeth marks all around the sides ... Hang on, Moss has seen something.'

Moments later Moss was looking up from the bottom of the chamber at Mec with a worried look on his face.

'Where the natural tunnel in the branch carries on towards your cave, there seems to be a small side cave, and in that are some large round things, like the eggs some of the flying lizards lay.'

'All right,' Mec called back, 'I'll just go back to my cave to get something, and I'll come down to have a look.'

He hurried off, to return moments later with his light making kit and a long thin knife. Sliding down the vine a lot faster than he intended to, he joined the others in the chamber and added a pinch of the two dried powders to the water in the transparent insect case of the light maker.

Moments later a soft glow of pale blue light lit up the chamber, getting brighter as Mec stirred it up with a stick.

'Now let's see what you've found, lead the way Moss and don't touch anything, there may still be a little of the fungus powder down here where the rain didn't reach.'

They stopped, open mouthed at what they saw. The creature had indeed laid a collection of eggs in a small cave-like opening at the side of the tunnel, and some of them were jerking about as if they might well be on the point of releasing their contents.

'We'll have to roll the eggs out into the main tunnel, so that when we open them the contents will flow away from the main chamber. Whatever you do, don't get any of the fluid from the eggs on yourselves, oh, and don't touch the eggs with your hands, use a stave.'

Between them, they rolled all the eggs which showed no sign of internal movement out of the side chamber and down the tunnel towards the main tree trunk.

The remaining four eggs which were twitching as if they were going to open at any moment, were added to the end of the line in the tunnel, and all concerned stood back to survey their handiwork.

'Well, it looks nice and neat.' commented Mec, 'Now we have to destroy them, and carefully. If any of the eggs look as if they have a nearly mature creature inside them, you will have to kill it, otherwise just crack the eggs open and let the contents run out.'

They looked at one another to see who was going to begin the slaughter, and as there were no volunteers for the job they drew lots for the unpleasant task. Kel got the short twig, and picking up one of the bladed staves, made his way carefully along to the furthest egg in the tunnel, and drove the sharp blade into it.

There was a soft plopping sound as the thin leathery skin split open and a mixture of red fluid and brown lumps of something a little more solid spilled out onto the tunnel floor. Kel jumped back in surprise, tripped over the end of his stave and came crashing down between the next two eggs in the line.

The speed with which he regained his feet surprised them all, and he stood there shaking for a while before slashing the next egg, this time standing well back as the turgid contents surged out.

All went well, until the last egg in the line before the four which looked as if they were going to spew forth their living monsters.

As Kel drove in the stave, the egg almost exploded as the addled contents propelled themselves out in a fountain of foulness. The stench was overpowering, and they all fled to the main chamber to get some fresh air, which by the time they got there, falling over each other in the process, wasn't as fresh as they would have wished.

'Someone else can finish off the last four.' said Kel, his eyes streaming tears from exposure to the pungent reek of the rotten egg.

'All right, Moss and I will destroy the last ones. Moss, you slash the egg open, and I'll use the knife to finish off whatever we find inside it.'

There was no great rush to complete the job, but they were spurred on in their endeavours by the increasing stench which Kel had released upon them.

Moss split open the first of the wriggling eggs, and as he did so, the ugly head of a miniature version of the creature they had disposed of earlier reared up from the torn casing, complete with a vicious set of teeth, and looking for something to set them in.

Mec jumped forward and with one swing of the long blade, severed the head of the hideous creature from the body which was struggling to enter their world.

As Moss lifted the stave to make the opening incision in the last egg, it egg split open of it's own accord and a snapping head took the end of his stave off, leaving him with the shortened stump which he instinctively thrust into the gaping jaws and then jumped back, all in one fluid motion, knocking Mec flying in his efforts to reach safety.

By the time Mec had scrambled to his feet and joined the now shaking Moss, the creature had released itself from the confines of the egg case and was writhing about on the floor of the tunnel, trying to make sense of its new surroundings and bite anything within range.

Mec ran forward, grabbing a bladed stave from Kel as he passed, and began taunting the creature with it. At just the right moment when the tooth-laden head was about to strike, Mec thrust the stave into its mouth and then put all his weight behind the next thrust, driving the sharp end straight through the back of the creatures neck and pinning it to the wall of the tunnel, the claw tipped arms desperately trying to reach its tormentor.

'Pass my long knife!' Mec called, a touch of panic in his voice. 'Quickly!'

It took two swings of the razor sharp knife to sever the gyrating head from its body, which lay snapping its teeth on the floor of the passage.

'There's nothing more to do here now,' Mec gasped, trying to get his breath back, 'I'll come down here again tomorrow when the smell has gone to see if there are any more egg piles, but I don't think there will be.'

'I wonder if these creatures have a mate as we do?' asked Kel, but before he could get an answer, Mec was already making a fast and undignified exit from the chamber, climbing hand over hand up the vine as fast as he could, followed by the others as the import of Kel's question went home.

Having retreated to the safety of the open trackway and snatched a few lungs full of fresh air, the troop relaxed a little, exchanging nervous giggles and comments on the operation they had just completed.

'That's something I wouldn't like to have to do every day.' Kel said, wiping their weapons on a convenient patch of moss at the side of the path.

'But it looks as if we shall have to get used to doing it a few more times before we can be sure we are free of these creatures.'

'That won't be your problem, it's now up to the rest of the groups to defend themselves, you two have a much more important task ahead.' Mec made it a statement rather than a comment by his tone of voice.

'Do you really think the others will be able to do what we have just done?' asked Moss.

'They'll have to, if they want to survive.' Mec turned to the two supernumeraries,

'How do you two feel about taking on the job of ridding us of these pests?'

'I think we could, if you're there to guide us.' one of them replied, but without much conviction in his trembling voice.

'Hmmm.' was all Mec said.

They all stood around in silence for a while, perhaps a little annoyed at the lack of response from the supernumeraries or just because there was little else to say of any great significance after what they had been through.

'I think we all deserve a little something special after that escapade.' Mec said as he gathered up his equipment, 'Come on back to my place and I'll see what I can find.'

The little gang of monster killers trooped off behind him feeling satisfied with their day's work, and wondering just what the morrow would bring.

Arriving back at the tree cave, there was a definite taint in the air, and Mec tracked it down to a small hole in one of the side rooms.

'I think it must connect up with the tunnel in the main branch,' he said, wrinkling his nose, 'and I don't like the sound of that one bit.' The others crowded in to see what all the fuss was about, and they too agreed that the room didn't smell as sweet as it should.

'You'll have to plug it up or you'll lose all your friends.' said Moss, ever the jolly one, 'Or move home,' he added as an after thought.

Mec brought out some of the special wrinkled black berries he had offered to Kel on an earlier visit, and was much amused at the look on the faces of his guests as they saw the strange fruit swell up in the water to form a plumptious deep purple sphere, and the look of astonishment when they actually bit into them.

'The Greater Sun will be fading soon, so I think you should all be going back to your own groups before long as I have a few things to do before I retire for the day.' It was a command rather than a suggestion from Mec, and as they all respected his authority the party broke up, but not before Mec had told Moss and Kel to return on the morrow.

The journey back to the group was uneventful and they hadn't been missed. When Kel tried to tell some of them of the days exploits, there was little interest shown, his companion saying very little to back up the tale.

During the time of the Lesser Sun another member of the little group disappeared without trace or explanation, and no one seemed to care. Next day, as the Greater Sun broke through the green canopy above, two more youngsters were born, and so the group's numbers were sustained.

Kel found it hard to come to terms with this uncaring attitude of his group, to his way of thinking, they were in a permanent daze or stupor and wondered why he wasn't.

On his way back to Mec's tree cave, Kel stopped to look down into the hole left in the main branch after yesterday's removal of the creature and the egg destruction. The stench was just as bad, and a large amount of the trackway bark had been ripped away exposing the bare wood underneath. The tree would repair itself in time, but he wondered what horror would occupy the hole left in it.

Mec seemed his old self again after the trauma of yesterday, and they soon got down to the questions and story answers of old, which as usual, prompted even more questions from Kel.

When Moss joined them a little later, Mec sat them both down to impart a little more of his knowledge and said,

'There are one or two more tales I think you should hear before you set off on your adventure, the first being about the forest we live in. As far as we know, that is all there is, just forest for as far as anyone has ever gone, with of course the areas of the Death Sands, but according to legend, it wasn't always so as I shall relate to you.' He paused, as if wondering if he should go on, settled back on his gourd stool, took a deep breath, and continued,

'The old legends tell of great areas of coldness, where water goes hard at certain times, and others where it is hard all the time, a bit like the hard water pellets which occasionally fall from the forest top.'

'What I don't understand about that story is how could anyone live there if they couldn't drink because all the water is hard, and therefore how could such a place become known about. But it is only a story, and maybe not all true. If you should come across such a place and have to go into it for any reason, then you will find that the fine fur covering you have will not be enough to keep you warm. One possible thing you could do is to kill a creature which has a thick fur covering, skin it, and make yourselves a covering to keep you warm, it's only an idea, but may come in useful, should the need arise.

'And then there is the legend of the lands of fire, what ever that is. It is said to be very hot there, like it is when you go to the top of the forest when the Greater Sun is high in the sky, but even more so. It is said that it is so hot that nothing grows, and there are no trees or even remains of them, just sand and lots of stones. An even more preposterous tale is that in some places the very stones are so hot that they are in a liquid state, like thick water, and flow along the ground.

'Then there is the tale of great pools of water so big that you can't see the other side of them, and it is said that the giants travelled over these huge pools to visit other lands, in things called bots or boots, I'm not sure which. These are only legends, but there must be some truth in them, if only a little, so it is important that you should remember them in case you come across these strange things, and you will then know what dangers to expect.

'I have made up a little collection of things which I think will be of help to you on your journey of discovery, and you should take great care of them, for once lost, they can't be replaced. Do not be afraid to try out new ideas, but be careful, and observe all the effects caused by trying out something new, for from such things new ideas are born.'

Mec passed around the bowl of food things, giving the two listeners a chance to digest a little of what he had said.

While they were eating, Mec went into one of his smaller rooms, returning with armfuls of equipment he had collected and made, and laid them down on the floor of the main cave.

'I have made new belts for you to hang your equipment on, and now I'll go through the items I have collected for you, explaining what they are for.

'First, you have the new Greater Cutting Knives, these are very sharp and should last you a lifetime if taken care of. Next there is the light making thing. All you have to do is add a little of each powder to the water in the container, and stir it up. When the light fades a little, just stir it again and it will brighten. Only use it when really necessary as there is no way the powders can be replaced, unless you come back here!' The two lads looked at each other, the idea of not returning hadn't occurred to them.

'There is a good supply of the black berries which swell up when placed in water. Only use them when you can find no other food to eat, and then only one, or two at the most, at any one time. I have tried your suggestion of making a transparent cover for the direction indicating bowl, and it works very well. There is only one of these, so take very good care of it, as it is the only means you have of knowing that you are travelling in a straight line. A small selection of Lesser Cutting Blades without their handles are included for you to make your own weapons should you need to.'

Reaching down to the pile of artefacts Mec withdrew a wrinkled skin-like thing, and held it up.

'This is made from the skin of one of the creatures from the levels above us, and is intended to be filled with water if you think you may have to go through an area where there is none, and I suspect you may. All you do is open this end.'

With a twist and some effort he pulled a small well fitting wooden plug out of the neck-like end of the bag.

'And then push the whole thing into the water, keeping the opening near the surface. It will fill up with water and then you push the wooden plug back in. When not in use, it folds up quite small and goes into this little pouch on your belt. You may never need it, but I have tried to think of everything which might come in useful, based on what I know of the legends.

You will, of course, have the blade tipped staves, and should you break or lose them, you can make more from the spare blades in this pocket.' He indicated a bulging little bag attached to the belt.

'How long it will take you to find the edge of the forest, that's if there is an edge, and go into other lands, I don't know. But if you can return here one day and relate your adventures, it will greatly help me to bring some of the old stories up to date and make them a little more accurate for the future.'

Kel and Moss were quite overcome by all the attention which Mec had paid to their survival equipment, and didn't quite know what to say for a moment.

'Of course we will come back to tell you how we got on, and of any discoveries we make, that's if we survive the journey in the first place.' Kel said at last.

'There are two other things on your survival belt, as I now like to think of it. One is a small bag containing several smaller bags made from the thin skins of snapper bags, which may come in useful if you have to collect things. The other is a bag containing lots of little odds and ends, the sort of things I would like to have with me if I was going on such a journey. They may be helpful to you, and as they take up so little room, I would suggest that you accept them.'

'Do you have one more spare bag I could have, Mec?' asked Kel, and then proceeded to tell him of the 'Tinkle Stones' he had made and what they were for.

'I'm sure I have, where did you get them?'

'I twisted the fibrous threads from a plant stem, letting it dry in the sun so that it kept the twist in, and then hung from it at intervals, using the fluid from the Stave Plant, pairs of little stones and shells. The shells I found in the bottom of one of the larger Water Plants. They belong to a little creature which crawls about at the bottom of the pool, and some must have died or been eaten, for I found the shells empty. I don't know where the stones came from originally, I found them in a hollow recess in a tree near our group. No one seemed to know who they belonged to, so I took them.'

Mec stroked his chin thoughtfully, as if trying to remember.

'The stones must have come from the forest floor, it's the only place I know of where they can be found. Someone at some time must have brought them up here, and either forgotten about them, or died. I expect they would be pleased to learn of the good use you have put them to. I think I shall make a string for myself, it could guard the cave entrance for me at the time of the Lesser Sun.'

It was decided that on the morrow, the two travellers would set out on their adventure, first telling their friends in their respective groups what they were going to do. Kel said he didn't think there was much point in doing that, as no one seemed to care what anyone did in his group, and Moss added that it was much the same in his.

'Why do you think they are like that?' asked Kel.

'It has always been so, at least as far as I know, but every now and then, people like you two turn up and they have a different attitude to life, and that is what makes them special and able to go on the journey I have suggested.'

'I do wish more people were like you two, we could all survive far better then. The forest is changing and new life forms are appearing, you may not notice it, but I am much older, and I have seen the changes. I can see a time, when as a people, our groups will not be able to take care of themselves, and then they will be no more, and that is sad.' There was a note of deep sorrowfulness in Mec's voice.

'Well, let's see what we can find,' said Moss, 'there may be something out there which will change things. Who knows what we'll discover. There could be another race of people like us but with a bit more interest in life, and if we can bring the two groups together, it may well benefit us all.'

Mec looked thoughtful for a few moments, and they waited patiently for him to gather his thoughts, and tell them more.

'According to the old legends, and they are very, very old, there used to be many different races of people in this world, and the differences you would find hard to believe. It is said that they had different coloured skins, some were very tall, while others were short, but I don't know how their sizes related to ours. It would seem that some were very clever, and they were responsible for all the wondrous things that were made, and we think this lead to their consequent downfall. The clever ones appeared to control the less clever ones, who were quite content to just live a simple life, rather like your own groups, I would think. A lot of the stories were so unbelievable that over time, they were not told any more, at least, that's what my Story Teller told me.'

Mec paused, as if deciding whether to say any more.

'There is one story I heard from a Story Teller from another group, when I was young like you, but I find it hard to believe. Long long ago, the clever people made a travelling device which would take them up to the Lesser Sun and they were able to get out and walk about on it!'

'I know, it's hard to believe, and I for one think that the story may have been added to over the years in the telling of it, and something else really happened which has been totally forgotten. But then again, it could well be true, as may some of the other seemingly impossible stories. Perhaps you might come across another Story Teller from another group, and then you could get him to relate some of the stories he has.'

'But if they were so clever, why did they destroy themselves and everything they had made?' asked a baffled Moss,

'You are more clever than us, and we are more clever than the other members of our groups, but we wouldn't destroy what we have, let alone ourselves.' Kel too, could make little sense of what appeared to have happened so long ago.

'Perhaps if you meet other Story Tellers, you might get some answers to your questions about the old times, and if you do, I would very much like to know what you find out. But that is enough of the old tales, we have other more important things to talk about.' Mec was keen to arm his young travellers with all the knowledge he thought might be useful.

They talked on, covering all the possible dangers which Mec thought might be out there in the unexplored world he felt sure existed beyond the confines of the forest. Several more of the old legends were told, each holding some item of interest for the forthcoming expedition, until it was time for the two youngsters to leave for their own groups, and retire for the coming time of the Lesser Sun.

If the truth be known, neither slept too well that night as the level of excitement reached a high point neither of them had ever experienced before, and even Mec found himself going over the things he had said, to make sure everything had been fully covered.

During the hours of darkness Kel's 'Tinkle Stones' sent forth their musical warning notes, and he leapt to his feet from half sleep with the blade tipped stave in his hand. There was nothing there that he could see, just the gentle beams of the Lesser Sun painting the surrounding trees in its silvery light, the only sound being the occasional snore from a group member, deep in sleep and oblivious to the rest of the world.

Kel couldn't get back to sleep properly, and spent the rest of the night trying to imagine what the next day would hold for them, and would they actually survive 'till the following night.

In this half awake, half dream like state, he drifted through the hours of darkness, his imagination running riot every now and again causing him to snap wide awake, looking for that which had jolted him out of his night time world of fantasies.

Three:
The Journey Begins

He was up and about long before the rest of the group, gathering his early morning meal and consuming it in great haste. There wasn't any point in hanging about, saying goodbye or any of the other things he had thought he should do. The journey couldn't begin soon enough for him, and as soon as he had finished eating he cleared up his resting place, collected his few belongings and headed off for Mec's cave, and a new life, he hoped.

Despite his early rising, an even keener Moss had preceded him by some few moments, and greeted him with a cheery, 'Couldn't you sleep either?' and a big grin.

Mec had all their expedition equipment ready in two neat piles, and as they entered the tree cave he came forward to greet them.

'I so wish I were young and coming along with you two, but someone has to stay home and look after things. He said. 'Although I sometimes wonder if it's worth all the effort.'

Mec showed them how to secure their carry belts, and then attach all the items he had prepared for them. The new Greater Cutting Knives were the last items to be handed over, and this was done with some degree of reverence, as they were very special things indeed.

'If I may, I would like to show you how to use the Direction Finder once more to be sure that you have understood the principle.' Mec took the little bowl with its transparent top, and placed it on the floor.

'You see the little black stick with the white blob on the end, it will always point in the same direction no matter where you are. As you can see, it is now pointing in the direction the Greater Sun will take up at midday meal time, and that is the way I think you should go.'

'If you want to veer off to one side for any reason, then you only have to make a mark on the rim of the bowl, and using the floating black stick you can see if you are going in the desired direction.'

Both Moss and Kel had already well understood the way the Direction Pointer worked, and hid their impatience to get underway out of deference to the older man. Finally fully kitted up, the pair stood outside Mec's cave, eager to be on their way, but somehow loath to leave the old man.

They could see the longing in his eyes to be joining them, and the loneliness he would feel when they had gone, but there was nothing they could do about it. It was the way things were.

There were a few moments of embarrassed silence, and then Mec came forward, embracing each of the travellers in turn and wishing them well. Just a glint of a tear showed in Mec's eyes as the pair turned away from him and strode out along the main branch towards the next massive rising tree trunk, away in the distance.

Halfway along the branch, Kel turned to wave a final goodbye, but the Story Teller was nowhere in sight, having returned to the loneliness of his tree cave and his even lonelier thoughts.

The day was young, and Moss broke into a slow trot out of sheer exuberance, following the well worn path along the branch, with Kel in hot pursuit.

Soon the next big rising trunk was reached, and they carefully edged their way around it and were on to the next branch which was a very long one, disappearing off into the wisps of rising morning mist from the forest below.

Two trunks later and the pathway was no more, there being no sign of wear due to feet padding along on the quest for food or anything else.

'We'd better take a little more care now,' said Kel, 'as this branch hasn't been used by the look of it, and we don't know if it's safe.' Moss agreed, and the pace was reduced to a steady walk, both explorers looking from side to side for anything which might threaten them.

Halfway along the next branch their way was barred by a curtain of Whip Vines, hanging down from the dizzy heights above and forming a solid screen of twitching tendrils, each one capable of dealing a death blow if given half a chance.

'That's a good start to our adventure.' commented Moss, seemingly unperturbed at the sight.

'It could hold us up for some time, as we will have to cut so many of them down, and then wait for the juice to dry on the branch before crossing the area' Kel added.

'Not for very long.' Moss called back as he reached up with his blade tipped stave, and brought the first of the vines crashing down like a live writhing snake, to slip over the edge of the branch and go twirling and twisting down to the forest floor so far below.

They had cleared a small passageway through the curtain very quickly, allowing just enough room for them to pass the nearest vines without stimulating them into their lethal action of whipping out sideways and encompassing anything within reach.

'The branch is soaking wet with the juice,' Kel said, 'and will take ages to dry.'

'Doesn't matter,' Moss replied, 'we can still get though. See that big plant over there in the crotch of the main branch and the side one? Well the leaves are harmless, so if we cut some down, pile them up and put them over our heads it will protect us from the dripping juice, and then as we go forward, we take them off one at a time, turn them over and place them on the branch to cover up the juice.'

'Wish I'd thought of that.' Kel mumbled to himself as he cut the first giant leaf down.

It didn't take them long to work their way through the wriggling curtain of death, and were soon out the other side, none the worse for the chance they had taken.

'Just in case you thought I had made that little trick up on the spur of the moment, it has been the normal way of dealing with the Whip Vines in my group for some time now, as we have a lot of them in our area.' Kel felt a little better for having been told that, and showed it with a nod of his head.

Several more rising main trunks and their lateral branches later, Kel called for a rest. The packs they were carrying were not very heavy, but they were not used to even that little extra weight, and found it tiring.

'How far do you think we shall have to go before we come across a change in the forest? Moss asked, 'Not that I'm bored with our travels, as there is always something different to see.'

'I don't really know, but the first thing would probably be one of the Death Sand patches, according to our Story Teller, or maybe some unknown new life form.'

As the Greater Sun was now nearly overhead, they decided to scout around for their midday meal, and soon had a collection of fruits and berries piled up on the branch.

'Must say, this is more interesting than what I was doing before.' said Moss.

'And what was that,' asked Kel.

'Nothing much.' and they both laughed out loud, sending several creatures scurrying for cover who were not used to such a noise.

Having taken their meal, the pair were on their feet again and heading out in the same direction Mec had suggested, having first checked with the Direction Pointer to make sure.

By late afternoon, they had long ago left the forest they knew, and several new plants appeared on the branches, although the trees themselves seemed the same.

The Water Plants were still in abundance as were many of the fruits they were familiar with, so food and water were no problem, but would not remain so for much longer.

The Greater Sun suddenly lost its light quickly, and this usually heralded a rain storm.

'Let's cut some of those giant leaves down so that we can shelter under them, as I see no point in getting our things or ourselves wet.' It was Moss's turn to look surprised at Kel's suggestion, but they both set to with a will to collect enough leaves to keep them dry, and a few left over.

'Why not put the leftover leaves around the sides, so hiding us from anything which might come along.' suggested Moss.

'Two good new ideas in one day is a bit too much.' replied Kel with a chuckle, arranging the spare leaves to form a box-like structure around them, and only just in time as the first large rain drops began to fall.

It was just as well they had made some kind of shelter, for the storm raging overhead was one of the worst in living memory.

Lightning ripped through the upper levels, setting fire to some of the trees which had died, but had been held up by their neighbours for so long.

Flaming fire brands whizzed past them, and twisting their way down through the canopy from trees which had exploded when the lightning struck their wet cores, sending showers of sparks in all directions.

The two travellers cowered beneath their leaf shelter, dry for the time being, but shocked by the cacophony of sounds which assailed their ears and the unusually heavy deluge of water.

The screech of creatures even more terrified than the sheltering pair, rent the air, mingled by the echoes of the trees ripped asunder by the force of the storm, and the terrible power of the electric discharges.

There was nothing they could do but wait out the storm, and wonder what had happened to their groups who would be soaked by now, and running about like scared Screech Birds and probably falling off the wet and slippery branches.

Having spent it's fury on the forest top, the storm slowly moved away, only the soaking wet vegetation and the plumes of smoke rising up from the fire brands which had landed on wide branches and not made it down to the forest floor told of the destruction which must have occurred in the upper levels.

Finally the rain stopped, with occasional large drips descending from the foliage above as leaves bent under the weight of water they had trapped, sending their loads cascading ever downwards.

'Well, we're dry at least. And probably the only two things in the forest which are,' Moss added, 'except possibly Mec, I doubt if anything catches him by surprise.'

'It would have to be up very early in the morning to do so.' responded Kel.

They set about rearranging the giant leaves to hide their presence completely, and then Kel suggested that they took it in turns to keep watch and sleep, just in case something they were not used to came along.

Just before the dawn broke, something large and rustley came by, and Kel who was on watch touched Moss on the arm to wake him. They both stood, hidden in their leaf hideout with blade tipped staves at the ready, but whatever it was passed them by. Neither of them slept any more that night.

The first meal of the new day went down well, and both were in a cheerful mood. The branches had dried out during the night, and they hadn't been eaten, or even bitten for that matter.

'Things can only get better after that storm.' Kel offered as a conversational opening piece, but Moss had his mouth too full to do more than just nod his head and do his best to grin without spilling too much juice from the fruit he was eating.

Soon they were on their way again, after first checking that the Direction Pointer and that they were on the correct heading. The branches between the main rising trunks were getting longer and thinner, although they were still wide enough for a safe path to be trodden, and the pair hurried along aware that something had changed, but were not sure what it was.

Moss suddenly gave the signal to stop, and Kel nearly ran into the back of him as he had been looking the other way when Moss raised his hand in silent signal. After they had disentangled themselves again, Moss said,

'I know what it is, we must be getting closer to the Greater Sun, it's a lot lighter here.'

'Or the top of the forest is not so high above us now.' retorted Kel, who long ago had realized that the Greater Sun was always the same distance away, and the light level depended on how high up in the forest you were.

'Yes, could be.'

They hurried along the now thinning branch, eager to see what other changes there were to be found which Mec had not told them about, or even knew of himself. They were not disappointed. Suddenly, the Greater Sun burst forth upon them, causing them to shield their eyes against the glare, and stop in their tracks.

As their eyes got used to the increased light level, they could see that the forest was thinning out to a few wispy trees which were nothing like the ones they had been travelling through, and in the distance they could see a great area of yellow sand.

'That must be the Death Sands Mec told us about. He said we mustn't go any nearer than we are now, this is where the trees change to those ugly looking stumpy ones, and they lead right down to the Sands themselves.' Kel wasn't one for taking chances.

'We'll have to go around them then, that's if we want to carry on in that direction.' Moss said, a little disappointed that they would have to go some distance before they would again be heading in the correct direction according to Mec's instructions.

They turned and back tracked some way until the trees looked a little more familiar, and then reset the Direction Pointer to take them east of the Death Sands, and hopefully past them.

Speeding on, now that they were on wider branches, the pair had covered a considerable distance when they stopped for the midday meal, and it was as they did so that the next surprise in store for them became evident.

In a clearing just ahead, a giant block-like stone reared up into the sky, tree branches growing into and through the holes which were dotted about its surface.

'Do we eat, or go and have a look?' asked Moss, with a slight hesitation in his voice.

'Eat first, in case we have to run for it and feel faint from lack of food.' Kel replied, sensibly.

They ate, but not with the enthusiasm that usually accompanied the meal time, the strange block ahead had taken their interest above all else.

'All right, let's go carefully, there may be something unpleasant in there, and it may not have eaten as we have.'

As they approached the great stone monolith, a silence descended upon the area. There were none of the usual sounds of the forest, the little rustles and squeaks, the odd scream as something larger ate something smaller and then belched.

'If we go along that branch, we will be able to go into the same hole the branch goes into, and if we don't like what we see, it will be easy to get out again quickly.' Moss took the lead, and they cautiously entered the block.

'It's like a kind of tree cave, only very much bigger.' Moss called out, his voice strangely echoing around the huge space, causing the hair on his back to stand up.

'I can climb down this side branch and reach the flat level below. If I'm careful.' he added as an afterthought.

Some moments later they were both on the flat surface of a giant room, with square walls on every side and a big opening in two of them. Going over to one of the holes in the wall, they were surprised to find another huge room, and what looked like even more rooms leading off that one.

'It looks as if it's made of stone, but I've never seen stone of this size before, and so flat. Stones are usually rough or knobbly or even round, or at least, the ones I've seen brought up from the forest floor were.' said Moss, running his hand over the nearly smooth surface.

'I wonder if this is a leftover from the time of the giants which Mec was telling us about, 'cos it looks as if it has been made rather than brought about by nature.'

'This place doesn't feel right.' a nervous Kel commented as they walked from room to room, 'I don't think we should be here, there's something about it which makes me feel very uneasy.'

'Why are there so few leaves on the surface we are walking on, where have they gone? It should be knee deep in droppings from the trees I would have thought.'

As Moss didn't have answer for that, he remained silent. They finally lost their collective nerve when they came to a huge dark hole which went down to what they assumed would be the forest floor. A cold dank smell wafted up every now and again, and the inky blackness below them seemed to have a strange beckoning effect, as if something wanted them to jump down the shaft.

'Come on,' said Moss, 'we should be all right as long as we keep our wits about us, let's go as far as we can to see what's at the end of this place. As long as we have a branch to climb out on, we should be safe enough.'

They walked on from to room to room until an opening far larger than the square ones in the walls came into view.

'This looks like the end of it.' said Moss, fearlessly going up to the huge gap in the otherwise flat walls.

'This is different, it looks as if the stone has been melted and run down the side of the place.'

'But what could melt stone?' asked an incredulous Kel, running his hand over the smooth glassy surface, 'It looks as if it has turned into a liquid, run down a little and then suddenly gone hard again, but that's surely not possible.'

Moss looked in a pensive mood for a while, and stroked the smooth glassy runnels of fused artificial stone.

'Mec said we would find a lot of things that would be strange and unfamiliar to us, and this is one of them. I think this is a thing made by the giants of long ago, and something has happened to this end of it, as it is different to the rest.' he paused for a moment, 'The Death Sands are not far away. Let's check the Direction Pointer to see where we are compared to the point where we turned back earlier on.'

They set the little bowl down on the floor, and the black stick swung around several times before coming to rest.

'It's as I thought,' said Moss, 'the Death Sands must be over there,' pointing with an out stretched arm, 'and this side of the place faces in that direction, so I think the Sands have something to do with this runny looking stone here.'

'It must have been a greater hotness than the Greater Sun could ever produce, even on a very hot day, so what could it have been?' Kel was now getting interested in the matter.

'I don't know, but Mec did say something about the Great Lights, perhaps they were very hot, and did this.'

'Like the Streaky Lights we see in the forest top when there is a storm.' said Kel, trying to relate the situation to something he knew.

'Possibly, but maybe even stronger. You're right, there is something about this place which doesn't seem right, perhaps we'd better leave it now and go on our way.'

They retraced their steps until they came to the branch they came in by, and returned to the more familiar surroundings of the forest.

Using the Direction Pointer to make sure they were still on course, the pair set off to hopefully circle around the edge of the Death Sands, and then continue their journey south.

Two days later, while trotting along an unusually long branch, Moss called a halt.

'Can you hear that?' he asked, 'It's almost like the noise a storm makes, but it doesn't stop. I can feel it in the branch, through my feet.'

The branch was vibrating very slightly to the rhythm of something in continuous motion and even the very air seemed to tremble as they looked around to see what was causing the disturbance.

'I've also noticed this branch is getting very much thinner as we go along it, but as it doesn't move it must mean that the other end has joined up to a rising trunk somewhere.'

'I hope it has.' rejoined Kel, not looking forward to retracing their steps for such a distance.

They continued along the trembling branch for a while until something made Moss stop again in mid stride. Silently pointing to large bulge in the branch and very quietly said,

'Snapper Bag, and it's big. I've never seen one this size, although I know they come in all sizes, shapes and colours.'

Before them, completely blocking their progress was what looked like a large piece of the main branch, which had humped itself up into a ridge.

'We can't get past that,' said Kel, 'there's not enough space on either side of it to get by safely.'

'We'll have to move it then.' Moss replied, more in hope than anything else.

'Our Story Teller once said that someone had actually been swallowed by an extra large one of these, and his friends took a great risk by going around the back of it and slitting it open, dragging him out and throwing him into a very large Water Plant which was nearby. It saved him, and he lived on to a good old age, but was completely bald. The juices inside the Snapper Bag had dissolved all his hair and it never grew back again.'

Kel gave him a look which is usually reserved for tall stories, but Moss seemed quite adamant about it.

'One thing in our favour, they don't usually have teeth, just a bony rim around the edge of their mouths, so unless it can get a good grip on a large portion of one of us, we stand a good chance of escape should we get too near it.'

'Just what do you have in mind?' asked Kel, thinking the worst.

'Well, we can't risk going past it, to go back will take up a lot of time and energy, so we'll just have to move it somehow.'

'How can we possibly do that? It's far too big to push of with a stave, even with two of us pushing.' Kel was still a little worried as to what Moss had in mind, if anything.

'I can see only one way of getting rid of our friend, and that's to get him to take some bait on the end of a vine, and having swallowed it, try and jerk or pull him off the branch. I know he's a lot heavier than us put together, but I can't see anything else we can do.'

They both stood there, staring at the Snapper Bag, and the Snapper Bag stared back, without moving.

Moss went back up the main limb of the tree to look for a suitable vine he could cut down, while Kel went up a side branch searching for anything which would do for bait.

The vine was easily procured, but bait suitable for the Snapper was almost non-existent, as neither of them had seen any living creatures for some time, except the barrier in their path.

'Don't suppose it would go for a large fruit?' asked Kel.

'I doubt it.' Moss replied, as they lay in wait for something to past them, 'That means we need living food.' he added.

'Perhaps we could annoy it enough for it to grab the end of the vine.' Kel suggested, 'I don't think they move very fast, at least the ones I know about don't.'

'That's worth a try,' Moss responded, 'let's do that.'

They threw the end of the vine towards the Snapper, hitting it across the snout, but all they got for their trouble was a blink from one eye, the Snapper making no attempt to grab the vine as they had hoped.

They both walked back some way from the seemingly lifeless barrier to their progress, and sat down.

'We shall have to find something large and bulky to attach on to the vine and then one of us will have to jab the little beast on the nose with a bladed stave enough to hurt, and when it makes a grab for it, the other will have to try and drop the loaded vine into it's mouth. Having taken the bait, we should be able to move it, as I doubt if it can bring it up again once having swallowed it.'

The hunt for something to add to the vine only turned up some gourds, so they had to settle for them, attaching the ball-like pods in a small bunch as firmly as possible.

Moss looped the baited vine over the end of his stave and Kel advanced with the other stave held at the ready to jab the obstruction on the nose.

Several jabs later and no sign of the creature making a move to take the bait, they were ready to give up the attack, when Moss had another of his good ideas.

'We'll have to make the bait a little more interesting for it, so let's rub the gourds on our bodies so some of our scent sticks to them, and he might think it's a meal after all.' The gourds were rubbed over their sweat glands until their skin felt sore, and were then reattached to the vine.

Once more the pair advanced on the log like creature, but before they began to attack it Kel stopped short and said,

'If we loop the vine over that side branch and then pull it, the Snapper will be dragged over to one side of the branch, and maybe over the edge.'

'I like that idea.' Moss said as he threw the end of the vine high up into the air, and watched in satisfaction as it snaked over the branch above their heads and then end fell back almost into his grasp.

'Right, here we go again.' he added, and with that they both advanced once more towards the creature.

Two sharp jabs on its snout did the trick, the cavernous jaws flew open, Moss swung the baited vine across the toothless maw and the hard edged lips smacked shut, the bait safely inside.

Kel dropped his stave and ran over to the free end of the vine, taking up the strain until he could be joined by Moss, who had tripped over himself in his eagerness to jump back from the monster.

Together they heaved with their combined weights, doing little more than causing a slight movement of the creature's head from side to side.

'We'll have to climb up onto that small branch overhead, and then jump off holding the vine, that should jerk him over to one side of the branch.' said Moss.

Getting up to the required branch proved a little more difficult than they had anticipated, but they made it in the end, and prepared to do their death-defying leap to the main branch below.

'Don't forget, if we miss the branch, don't let go as we should swing back after a while.' and with this cheerful offering from Moss they both leapt out into space, the vine suddenly snapping taut, and the snapper being jerked almost to the curved edge of the main branch.

'One more go should do it.' said Moss, but before he could begin climbing up again, Kel stopped him with a hand on his shoulder.

'I've got a bad feeling about this, I think we should cut and attach another vine to ourselves, so that if the other vine breaks, we won't join our friend over there hopefully doing his flying exercise.'

'That's a good idea.' said Moss, and went to cut another vine, one end of which was tied off tightly to a side branch and the other around their waists.

'Now comes the tricky part,' said Moss, 'we'll jump once more, but this time we'll have to let go of the vine, because if he goes over the edge, we'll be shot up into the air and could land anywhere.'

They climbed up once more, took a deep breath and dropped. This time the front end of the snapper was lifted right off the branch and as it tried to regain its balance by swinging its rear end round, it rolled over the curved edge of the branch and began its long journey down to the depths below.

As the snapper plummeted down, the vine fairly sang as it raced over the branch above, lifting the two on the other end off their feet before they had a chance to let go. As they sped upwards and were about to hit the branch above, the vine snapped under the strain, and they too were on their way down. The safety vine to which they had attached themselves brought them to a sudden jerking halt, squeezing the breath out of them as they dangled freely in space, slowly swinging to and fro.

'If we build up enough swing, we should be able to get back onto the main branch.' Moss finally managed to gasp.

Like a pair of youngsters at play, they gradually built up enough momentum to swing themselves over to the main branch and a safe landing.

To prevent themselves swinging back out again, they grabbed a handful of Prickly Sticks, as these were the only things within their reach.

Having regained some degree of dignity after dumping their adversary overboard, the next task was to extract the thorns which they had picked up from grasping the Prickly Stick plant.

'That's as close to imitating a flying lizard as I ever want to get.' Kel said, spitting out yet another thorn.

'Well, at least we can get going again.' said Moss, having completed his thorn extracting exercise and looking around for something to eat.

After a quick meal, and a long drink from a nearby Water Plant, the two were on their way again, the branch getting ever thinner as they went.

'I've just realized something.' called Kel, who was several paces ahead of a more cautious Moss.

'Look down below, I think I can see the forest floor, it certainly looks like it, and the light is getting stronger as if we were going up into the next level, which I don't think we are. Therefore the forest must be getting shorter, so perhaps we are approaching the edge of it.'

'Not only that, but the deep rumbling sound is getting louder, so there's something new out there.' Moss's voice had an edge of excitement in it.

Before them, thin spirals of mist were drifting through the branches, obscuring a clear view of what lay ahead, while the branch they were on seemed to go on for ever, twisting and turning its way through the forest.

'We shall have to slow up a little, as it is getting too narrow for my liking.' called Moss, who had taken the lead. 'And the mist is getting even thicker,' Kel added, wondering where it came from.

At long last the rising trunk of a vast tree loomed up ahead of them, and both gave a sigh of relief having found the point where their branch joined up with the rest of the forest again, providing a resting place for the coming night.

Several branches broke out from the main trunk, forming a safe platform on which to rest, and it was a weary couple who settled down to eat and prepare for a good sleep, having spent most of the day on the move, and some of it under extreme exertion.

Kel, ever the curious one, had gone out onto one of the branches on the far side of the trunk, and called back to Moss, 'Come and look at this, you wanted something different, and you've surely got it.'

Ahead of the pair, seen dimly through the intervening leaf-laden boughs, was a massive cliff rising up towards the top of the forest. Only small portions of it were visible through the gaps in the greenery, but the overall continuity of it was obvious.

'If you thought the other stone place was large, how about this.' said Kel as Moss drew up alongside him, pointing towards the gigantic uprising of stone.

'Maybe this is where the forest ends, and some of the other lands Mec was telling us about begin.' offered Kel, eager to get Moss's view on the matter.

'It could well be, but he didn't say anything about these huge stone places, or anything like them.'

'I can see through the tree tops over there, and the air above is a pink colour, I hope this isn't the hot place he was talking about, we can't go there.' Kel had a disappointed tone to his voice, as he could foresee them going back to Mec with very little accomplished.

'Let's take a rest now, the light is getting less, and the whole thing may look different in the new light of the Greater Sun when it is high above us.' and with that, they returned to their resting site.

As there were no giant leaves to cut down in the vicinity to form a shelter, the string of Tinkle Stones was strung up to guard against any strange creatures creeping up upon them during the time of darkness, and then they settled down for a well earned sleep, taking it in turns to keep watch, as usual.

A tired Kel was kept awake by the strange sounds of the night as various monstrosities went about their business.

After the time of the giants, Earth had changed at a greater rate than ever before in her long history.

The vast amounts of energy which had been released caused huge volumes of water to vaporize, forming a cloud mass which reached from ground level right up into the stratosphere, blocking out all sunlight.

Weather patterns which were normally considered to be fairly chaotic, were even more so after the holocaust, with raging storms causing vast flash floods, sweeping away considerable amounts of the softer land masses into the now soup-like turbulent seas. Wind velocities in excess of two hundred miles per hour were not uncommon, while the enormous electric charges built up by the speeding cloud masses brought about lightning displays the like of which had never been seen before, although there were not many about to witness them.

The intense radiation permeated just about every living cell structure, bringing about DNA changes at an ever increasing rate, although most of the mutated forms resulting from this bombardment didn't survive for very long.

Some did, however, and it was from these new species that the slowly recovering earth was to be populated.

Eventually, after a very long time, the skies cleared, and as the ozone layer had been depleted almost to zero, cosmic radiation from the now very active sun spots bathed the earth, causing even more opportunity for nature to rearrange her DNA patterns, bringing about yet more mutant forms, only the strongest and most able surviving.

Where forests once stood composed of single trees standing proudly beside each other, the high winds decreed that only trees which could join together forming a solid group would be strong enough to withstand the onslaught. And so Kel's world came about, in time.

For a while the forest was bathed in the darkness of night, and then the Lesser Sun climbed the heavens, casting its silver beams upon the forest canopy, some of which filtered down to give the apparentcy of life to the writhing twists of the gyrating mist wraiths.

As the coolness of the dark time deepened, the mists thickened, blotting out most of the forest detail so that only looming indistinct shapes remained.

Only the deep rumble of something large and heavy, constantly on the move remained the same through the night, and had done so for a very long time.

The deep black of night gave way to greyness, and then as dawn broke, Moss gently woke Kel saying in a hushed voice,

'I think there's something out there, and it might be looking for the first meal of the day.'

They strapped on their carry belts, picked up the bladed staves and cautiously crept around the massive tree trunk to see what lay beyond.

The mists had thinned a little, but not enough to see very far into the greenery between them and the great stone cliff.

And then they saw it. A dirty grey coloured worm like creature of gargantuan proportions was slowly humping its way along a branch towards them, two pitch black slit eyes glaring out malevolently at them above a salivating wrinkled mouth which slowly opened and closed.

'Quick, this way!' yelled Moss, jumping across a small gap between two branches, 'it can't follow us along here.'

With Kel in hot pursuit, Moss raced along one of the thinner branches which they wouldn't normally have used, to reach the rising trunk of the next nearest tree.

'Now where?' from a shaking Kel.

'Just keep still and watch.' replied Moss.

'Where do we go from here?' asked Kel, looking around anxiously for some means of escape.

'We stay put, look at the branch just down there. It's had a side shoot at some time which has died and rotted out, this should have weakened the main branch, and with a bit of luck, it won't take the creature's weight.'

The monstrosity in dirty grey gradually came closer, slowing down as it reached the thinner portion of the branch, having difficulty in keeping its balance.

Much to their dismay, most of it's long body had passed the weakened section of the main branch when Moss yelled out, 'Quick, grab that bough and hold onto my hand, whatever happens don't let go.' and with that he leaped forward and jumped up and down on the branch just in front of the approaching nightmare.

There was a loud crack, the branch behind the giant worm no longer able to sustain the weight of the huge creature plus the extra stress generated by Moss, finally gave way with a ripping sound, and began its journey downwards.

The creature was holding on with only two of its many gripping appendages and Moss jumped back, looking for his bladed stave.

With a couple of quick thrusts he severed one of the creature's grippers, and it swung over to one side, emitting a terrible howling sound as it sensed it's end was near.

One more thrust from his stave on the remaining gripper, and it was on its way down to the forest floor.

Bouncing off several branches below and complaining loudly as it did so, the creature hit the ground below with a dull slushy thump, and split open.

They both looked at each other, still shaking slightly after their narrow escape, and then sat down in silence for a few moments to regain their composure.

But Moss wasn't idle for long.

'Look at that, the floor of the forest isn't so far down as we thought, we could easily get down there, and see what it's like.'

'What about all the terrible creatures that are supposed to be there?' Kel wasn't too sure he wanted to go down.

'If we watch to see what happens to that creature which just landed, we should have a pretty good idea.' replied Moss, an answer always handy.

They sat on the edge of the branch and waited to see what, if anything, would turn up for a feast on the remains of the worm creature, but nothing did.

'I think it's safe enough to go down there now, we have our staves and could soon get up here again if we have to.' Moss was determined if nothing else.

'All right, but let's be very careful, there may be things under the leaf litter we don't know about.'

Slowly they made their way down to ground level, the last part of the journey was made easy for them due to a series of gently sloping branches which took them to the forest floor.

'I want to see what that creature's like now that it's safe.' said Moss and set off in the direction he thought it should.

It didn't take them long to find the monster, the smell gave it away.

'I've never smelt anything like that before, and don't want to again.' was Kel's comment as they approached the slowly disintegrating hulk.

'It shouldn't be decomposing already, so what's going on?' Moss wondered aloud.

There was no doubt about it, the creature was turning into a thick stinking liquid which was dribbling out of the split carcass and soaking away into the ground.

As they got closer they could see that the hulk was undulating in a most unnatural fashion, rippling movements under the skin giving it a semblance of life.

Moss picked up a stick and gave the open split a poke and immediately the end of the stick was covered in a countless myriad of tiny wriggling worms.

'Where have they come from?' exclaimed Kel, peering closer at the writhing mass clinging to the end of it.

'Must be from the ground.' they both looked at each other, turned as one and ran flat out for the branch they had come down on.

Having gained what they assumed was a safe height, the pair paused for a while to get their breath back and consider just what they had seen.

'That was awful.' exclaimed Kel, examining his feet.

'I don't think you have to worry about them, the worms must have sensed that the creature was dead, otherwise nothing else would be able to live on the forest floor.'

'Well, we haven't seen anything else so far,' Kel replied, 'so maybe that's why.'

'I don't think I want to go down there again, anyway,' said Moss, his curiosity satisfied, 'so let's carry on with our journey.'

They climbed up a little higher until they had reached the point where they had done battle with the giant worm, and then resumed their trek in what they thought was the right direction, south.

'That rumbling noise is getting louder.' commented Moss, as they sped along the new network of branches, 'and it seems as if the ground is getting closer.'

'And the Greater Sun is getting brighter all the time.' added Kel, shielding his eyes as bright flashes of sunlight pierced the normal gloom of the forest.

The deep rumbling sound increased as they went along, until the edge of the forest as they knew it, came into view.

Peering out from the dense green foliage, they were confronted by the sight of an enormous cliff face, towering well up above the top of the tallest trees, and extending off into the distance in both directions for as far as they could see. They had to shield their eyes from the blaze of light from the naked Greater Sun.

Cascading down with a thunderous roar from the lip of the high cliff, was a column of water, breaking up as it fell into clouds of mist and spray to eventually crash down into a pool below. Raging turbulent currents swirled the water into a maelstrom of white crested waves, racing each other around the pool to finally exit into a broad river which flowed away to the South.

'I would never have believed this if I hadn't seen it.' exclaimed Kel, totally overwhelmed at the sight, 'I had no idea so much water could exist in one place, and look at the size of that pool.'

Together they stood there, marvelling at the massive cliff and the waterfall, and wondering what other sights lay in store for them.

'Let's check the Direction Pointer and see if we are still going the right way.' suggested Moss, and the little device was placed on a flat part of the branch. The needle pointed towards the cliff face, and the river which ran along beneath it.

'Do we go down to the water level and follow it, or do you think we should go up to the top of the cliff, and go along the top edge?' asked Moss.

'I think the cliff would give us a good view of anything which we should be aware of below it, whereas if we go down we will only see what is in front of us.' Kel replied.

They looked along the edge of the forest for the tallest tree which would take them as near to the cliff top as possible, and began the long climb up.

In a desperate effort to get above it's rivals, one tree had produced a long slim branch which almost touched the cliff face near the top, and the pair headed for it.

'It's getting a bit thin up here,' Moss called back to his companion as he crawled along the slender branch, 'we had better do the last bit one at a time.'

As Moss neared the end of the slim branch, it bent under his weight, and touched the rock face.

'Hold on tight, I'm going to climb onto the rock, and the branch will swing back.'

As Moss transferred his weight onto the cliff, the branch sprang up nearly catapulting Kel into the air, but he managed to hang on, and then began the long crawl towards the cliff and his friend.

'Climbing up here isn't going to be like climbing a tree,' Moss said, 'There are few handholds and its very slippery in places, also the light is hurting my eyes.'

But climb up they did, reaching the top in an exhausted state and very hot.

The view from the cliff top caused even more wonderment than the waterfall. It stretched into the far distance, a flat sand and pebble strewn plain with no trees or sign of other greenery. The river which fell in such splendour from the edge of the cliff, had cut a deep steep-sided gorge into the plain, and wound its way across the surface into the far distance like a wriggling snake, to disappear in the haze of the horizon.

'The water seems to be flowing to the South, and that is the direction we need to follow, so if we go along the edge of the water we should be all right.' Moss stated, and so it was.

They set off, following the edge of the gorge which became less deep as they went along.

'If the water turns to our left, we'll have to cross it somehow, and that could be a problem.' Kel said, 'I wish we had one of those bot or boot things Mec talked about from the time of the giants.' Moss made no comment, as he was deep in thought about food supplies if they should not find another forest, and that didn't look very likely.

They made camp for the night in a small depression at the edge of the gorge, which by now had shallowed somewhat, the water being only a short distance from them.

The stock of fruits and pods which they always kept topped up during their travels, would not last very long, as Moss commented, and another supply of food would have to be found, but what?

As the Greater Sun curved down to the horizon and the intensity of the light lessened, they were able to take in more of the finer details of their surroundings. The sand wasn't like that found in the Water Plants, being brighter in its many colours and sharper in texture. Smooth pebbles and rougher stones were scattered about all over the surface, indicating that the surface of the plain had been modified by water at some time, and then some form of upheaval had distributed the sharper edged stones around.

After eating, the pair settled down for the night, Moss taking the first watch and seeing the Lesser Sun rise above the horizon in it's silver white splendour.

Four:
The New Land

NOTHING TROUBLED THEM during the time of the Lesser Sun, except their own thoughts, and then they were awake again ready for the next section of their journey south.

When they left the area near the cliff edge, the plain seemed flat and featureless, but now there were slight undulations and small rises which were becoming larger as they progressed southwards.

The river was now almost level with the surrounding ground, and accessible for refilling their water bags which they kept topped up whenever possible.

Arriving at the top of a small rise, they saw the source of the river. A great upwelling of water seemed to come shooting right out of the ground from a vast circular hole, rising several times their own height before falling back to race on its way towards the cliff waterfall.

'Now that's interesting,' said Moss, 'if the water is coming out of the ground like that, then it must come from somewhere much higher up in order to spout out like that, because water always runs down to the lowest level, and there is nowhere in sight for it to come from. We can see out to the horizon almost, and there are no big rises in the ground, so how does it do that?'

'No good asking me.' Kel replied, a little annoyed that Moss should ask him such a question knowing full well that he couldn't answer it.

They stood looking at the magic water for a while, mesmerized by the strange effect, and then Kel realized that it at least solved the problem of having to cross the river.

'We had better fill all our water bags to the top before we go on,' Moss suggested, 'as we don't know if there will be another big flow of water like this, and we'll need extra for the dried berries, should we have to use them.'

With everything which would hold water full to the brim, they set off, skirting around the strange water spout, and back into line with the cliff edge, but some little way inland from it.

In the distance they could see the first really large rises in the ground, small hills with pieces of rock jutting out from their tops and the odd large boulder scattered about on the sand and pebble strewn plain.

As they drew nearer to the first of the small hillocks, the first plant came into sight, not that it would ever rival anything they were used to in the forest. Small, stunted, and not even a bright green like the plants which grew on the trees, it just sat there.

Its withered dull olive green foliage a pathetic sight, struggling to survive in an arid climate with little nutriment for its roots to gather from the barren sandy soil.

More plants appeared as they progressed along their way, none bearing fruit or berries as a possible food source. After three days and nights the terrain began to change again, some quite steep hills came into view and a carpet of rather straggly grass carpeted the shallow valley floors.

'Looking back to where we have come from, I'd say we were going down to a lower level,' said Moss, 'and that means we could come across the running water again.'

'Just as well, we don't have much left now and we will soon need some for soaking the black berries Mec gave us, as the fresh foods are nearly all gone.'

The hills began to tower over them as the valleys deepened, and more vegetation appeared, getting more diverse as they plodded on. The Direction Pointer was checked to make sure that they were still heading south, and the Greater Sun seemed to climb higher in the sky and grew hotter.

'I think I recognize this plant,' Kel exclaimed excitedly, 'it certainly looks like one which grew in the leaf litter caught up in the branches back in the forest. The pods are good to eat, but these ones are very small compared to those back home.'

'Do you think we should risk eating them?' Moss said, torn between the coming hunger and a full belly.

'Sooner or later we'll have to, so I'll take a little nibble and see what happens.' Kel pulled a small pod from the plants and bit into the end.

'It tastes the same, except that it isn't as sweet as the forest ones,' Kel pulled a face, 'and it's got a slight bitter taste. At least it's food I suppose.' he added, but not very enthusiastically.

Kel stripped the plant of all the better looking pods and stuffed them into one of the bags he had on his belt.

The quality of the grass improved as they went on down the valley, forming a soft cushion for their feet, and making walking much more pleasurable.

More and more plants appeared in the dips and hollows as they went on their way, none of which had the lush bright greenness of the forest variety, and few bearing any resemblance to those they were familiar with.

Two more days of trekking through the ever higher hills and deepening valleys brought them to the first sign of a tree since they had left the forest. It was a small stunted thing, but a tree nevertheless. They both went over to it and examined the trunk, which was only two or three times as thick as their own bodies.

'I feel almost sorry for it, out here all on its own.' Moss said, stroking the rough bark thoughtfully, 'It must have a bit of a struggle trying to survive without the support of other trees around it.'

'I'll climb up to get a better view from the top.' and with that Kel sprang up to the first of the lower branches and quickly gained the top.

'Come up and see this.' he called, the top of the tree swaying slightly under his weight.

The view from the top showed that the river had indeed returned, snaking its way around several hills and opening out like a silver ribbon below them, to cross the green plain below and disappear into the distance.

'There's something down there which is new.' Moss commented. 'It's like a series of small stone mounds, what do you suppose they are?'

'I don't know, never seen anything like them before. They must have been made by someone or something, as stones don't pile up like that on their own. We're too far away to see any detail, so let's go and have a look at them.'

They climbed down and set off in the direction of the mysterious stone piles, never guessing what they would eventually find.

It took them a lot longer to reach the stones than they thought, and before that the river had swung around and under the hillside they were going down, so they were able to replenish their much depleted water stocks, and for a moment the stone piles were forgotten.

With all the water containers full and having drunk well and washed most of the dust off their bodies, the pair were startled to hear a voice calling.

Looking back up the way they had come, they were more than surprised to see a lone figure running down the hill towards them.

As the distant figure drew a little nearer, Moss exclaimed, 'It's a female, at least I think so, and she looks a little different to us anyway.'

'Where came you from?' she asked, when she had got her breath back, 'you not of us.'

Moss responded to her query with his most beguiling smile,

'No, we come from a land far away, well over the other side of the great plain of sand and small stones, where there is a great forest, and we lived in it.'

'But them is bad lands, no one can cross them and live,' she said with a look of disbelief on her pretty face.

'But we are very strong, and we can.' Kel had drawn himself up to maximum height and expanded his chest to its fullest, not realizing that nature was taking a subtle hand in the proceedings.

'And what is a forest?' she asked, looking puzzled.

'It's a great collection of trees, like that one over there, but much bigger and many many more of them, all in a group. They are so tall that they almost reach right up to the Greater Sun.' Moss pointed to the brilliant white blaze above.

'That not be, they would fall over. Anyway, where would you place your hutt if you lived in trees?'

'We don't have hutts that I know of... what is a hutt?' it was Moss's turn to look puzzled.

She smiled sweetly at them, 'It is the place you live in, where you keep things, where the family lives, look, I show you,' and with that she walked off in the direction of the bend in the river, the two travellers in hot pursuit.

'Nice looking female.' Moss commented, as they tried to keep up with the fleet footed stranger, 'Better looking than most of ours.'

'Must say, I agree with you there.' added Kel, grinning.

As they panted around the bend, trying to keep up with their agile guide, several dark grey stone huts came into view, now looking much larger than they had before, and very solidly constructed.

Their guide ran into the largest of the huts, and quickly came out accompanied by four other people, one of whom was a much older female and the tallest of the group.

'You welcome to us.' the older female said, smiling down at the two. 'You come a long long way to see us. Come to my hutt, and take food.'

They all trooped into the stone building, and the pair was surprised to see things to sit upon and a big flat board on legs in the middle of the room.

'Please to sit down,' the older female said, pushing the three legged crude wooden seats closer to the table, 'I get you food.'

She produced several flat wooden boards laden with fruits, most of which the pair hadn't seen before, and were hoping they wouldn't have to eat.

'Are all of these good to eat?' asked Kel, not wishing to place himself at risk eating something he knew little about.

'All are good food. You do not have like these?' the older female asked.

'Not these.' said Kel, pointing out the ones he didn't recognize.

'All are good, you eat this.' and she handed him one of the ugliest pods he had ever seen. Taking a cautious bite from one end, he was pleasantly surprised at the sweet flavour and smooth texture, and the rest of the pod soon followed the first bite.

After they had eaten their fill, the old female smiled, saying,

'You tell about you selves, where you come from, how you get here, and why you want to get here.'

Moss and Kel took it in turns to tell the story in full detail from the day their Story Teller had suggested that they go on their journey, right up to the moment the young female came running up to them.

The listeners seemed surprised at the description of the forest life the two had led, and the length of the journey they had undertaken for seemingly little reason other than to just do it.

By now several other females had joined the party, and despite the size of the hut, it was getting crowded and a feeling of excitement was in the air.

While the older female was addressing the newly increased crowd, Moss slowly leaned forward, quietly saying to Kel,

'I don't like this, there's something going on which we are not aware of. They seem to know about it, but we don't, so watch out and be ready to make a run for it.'

'Now we tell you some of our life.' the older female had a commanding tone to her voice, and every one paid attention at once.

'We not have Story Teller like you, but I do the same kind of thing. I remember the old tales from long ago, and I tell them to us people. One time I tell them to the one who will be in my place when I go to the sky, and so the tales will go on to the new people.' She paused to see if that had been understood, and seemingly satisfied, carried on,

'A long time ago, a tall man came to us and said that if the men go into the forbidden zone and collected things, he would give them anything they wanted. Him a strange man, and not like us, for he had no hair on his body and a round shiny head. We think him ugly. We females not like him, and tell our men not to go. But they go to the forbidden lands and bring back the forbidden things, which we will not have in our hutts. And so the forbidden things were kept in a hutt way over there,' she pointed with her old withered arm out of the doorway towards the low hills in the distance.

'Not long after, we not have good children. Some have no arms, some no legs, some no hair, some die at birthing time.'

'And then we not have any childs. None. We think it maybe punishment for men going to forbidden lands. Some of them get very sick and die early, some lose their hair and look ugly. Some can no longer do the child dance, and so we have no more childs.'

Moss and Kel were not too surprised, for their Story Teller had warned them to keep well away from the Death Sands, and the forbidden zone sounded as if it was something similar.

'We have heard of a similar place, and we wouldn't go there, for we think it does something to people which is very dangerous. How do you know that it is forbidden, and what does it look like?' Moss wanted to see if he could find out anything more about the forbidden zone, so that he could recognize it in the future should they come across it.

'We not go there, so not know what it look like. The old tales say it is a dead place, nothing grows, and there are strange lights.' The old female was holding something back, but Moss couldn't see what it might be.

'You never go to a place like that?' asked the older female with a touch of eagerness in her voice.

'No, never,' They both replied in unison, Moss wondering if they should have replied so emphatically, for some reason.

Kel noticed that the young female who had found them in the first place, had now moved up close to him, and he could feel the warmth of her body and the heady musky smell coming from her hair.

It made him feel hot and awkward somehow, along with a strange stirring in his loins which he had not known before.

The older wrinkle-faced female with only half her allotted number of teeth, looked around the rest of the group as if making her mind up about something, and then turned to Moss and Kel with her best effort at a sweet smile and said,

'If we have no more childs, when we go to the sky, our people will be no more. We must have more, and our men not give us any because of the forbidden lands they have been to.' She looked hard at the two, wondering if they had understood her unspoken request. They hadn't.

'You two are strong young men, you could help us,' she blurted out at last, 'you could give us the childs we need, it would be easy for you, and is good fun too.'

Moss and Kel weren't too sure about that as they were too young for mating when they were back in the forest, and only had a hazy idea of what was involved.

'I think we are too young for that kind of thing.' Kel said, feeling the hot blush of manhood suddenly being triggered by a surge of hormones.

'When you big enough, you old enough.' was her sharp retort, and they both knew there was little point in putting up any resistance as the doorway out of the hut was now completely blocked by several larger females who looked as determined as the older one sounded.

'We give you food and drinks and shelter, for you have no hutts of your own, and you give us the childs, then you can go see the other lands you spoke of.' It was an order rather than a request, and seeing no way out of it at the present, they both nodded their heads in submission, for the time being.

In one last desperate attempt to stave off what seemed to be an unavoidable initiation into an early manhood, Moss said 'We don't know what to do, as we haven't yet been paired with any females from our group .....'

'You not need to know, we will show you.' said the older female with the wrinkles and a knowing smile.

Moss and Kel looked at each other, hoping that the other could think of a way out of the inevitable.

Fresh wooden platters of food were brought out from a recess somewhere in the hut, and lots of little gourd cups along with a very large gourd of some drink appeared as if by magic. Everyone tucked in, the drinking gourds of Moss and Kel being topped up as soon as they had taken a little.

They both found the drink very pleasant, slightly sweet and a full fruity flavour. Little did they know it had been fermented for a while, and although not very potent, would have an effect if consumed in any great quantity, which they were doing without realizing it.

As the Greater Sun began to slide down below the horizon, the party in the hut was in full swing. Everyone was eating, drinking and generally making merry.

Kel's newly found friend was snuggled up against him as if she would freeze to death if she didn't, while several young females were doing their best to hold Moss's attention by asking him questions about his life in the forest.

Both adventurers had by now imbibed enough of the fruit drink not to care very much what happened, so there was little resistance put up by either of them as they were led out of the main hut and began the long night of visits to the smaller huts of the rest of the group.

Finally, they both fell asleep locked in the arms of which ever female was lucky enough to have been deemed the last one for that night, and awoke next morning feeling tired, sore, and not a little confused.

Before they were too sure of what was happening, they were back in the large main hut and being confronted by the older female.

'That was good fun for you each.' she cackled, showing a semi-toothless grin, and Moss later told Kel he hoped he hadn't mated with the 'scraggy one', but couldn't remember if he had or not, much to his dismay.

'You must eat now, and replace your strength.' she said, replenishing the food platters with more fruit and pods.

Both realized just how hungry they were when they eventually came out of their sleepy stupor, and tucked in with a willingness which belied the size of their bellies.

Feeling full and bloated, and not a little tired, they were led out into the bright light of day to bathe in the strong light of the Greater Sun, while several strong looking young females stood around doing nothing in particular, but were always close to hand.

By midday, Moss and Kel had recovered from their previous nights exertions, and were feeling a little more refreshed. The fact that they were, in effect, being guarded by the females only caused them to wonder what was going to happen next.

'I don't think I could keep that up for too long.' was Moss's comment, looking around at the well muscled females who were keeping an eye on them.

'I don't think the normal mating thing is as strenuous as last night, as we are only supposed to have one mate instead of a whole series of them,' Kel interjected, 'anyway, I don't remember too much of it after the first few huts, which is probably just as well.'

Kel beckoned one of the females over to him with the intention of asking a few questions about the group, but she either didn't understand him or pretended not to. He tried several of the others, and eventually one responded to his smiling request, and came and sat next to him. This caused not a few dirty looks from the others, and then Kel knew that they had been instructed to keep an eye on the pair, but not to get involved.

'Where do you get your fruit and pods from?' was his opening gambit.

The female pointed over towards a low hill covered in a dark and broken rocky formation,

'Down there's a deep valley where the big water go, and it is full of trees and bushes of food things.' she said smiling,

'I show you, yes?'

'Yes, I would like that, can we go now?'

The female got up and extended a hand to Kel, helping him onto his rather shaky legs. Moss somehow staggered up, and they began to move towards the stony hill.

The other females immediately gathered round and stopped them, angry glances being given to the bold one who'd dared to make contact.

'You must wait here, I see if you can go.' one of the larger females said, and walked off in the direction of a hut.

She returned a little later to say, somewhat reluctantly,

'You go, we come too.'

The party trooped off, the larger female leading the way and the more brazen one having got Kel's attention, helping him along by holding his arm.

They climbed the stony rise and before them was a deep valley, full of trees with the river running through it. The sunlight glinting off the water where it had broken through the green coverage, gave a gentle peaceful appearance to the scene, and Moss and Kel visibly relaxed in the false security engendered by what they saw before them.

As the first low bushes and smaller trees were encountered, the little group went in single file, some females leading and the rest bringing up the rear, the brazen one holding onto Kel's hand as there wasn't room on the narrow path for them to walk side by side.

'Looks like you've found a friend,' Moss quietly said to Kel, with a grin, 'perhaps she missed out last night, and wants to be first in the line tonight.'

'You mean we do it all again tonight?' Kel looked a bit surprised at the suggestion, 'I don't think I could, I'm too sore.' Moss just extended his grin with a knowing wink, and strode on into the small forest.

The path widened, and they could see that the trees had been trimmed to make access more available, and probably boost the fruit crop, of which there was a plentiful supply.

The river was slow flowing and looked very deep when they came to it. Being only a little below ground level, it was easy to gain access to the water, and Moss asked if he could enter it to wash.

The females looked at one another, none wishing to take responsibility for the possible escape of their prizes if they let them out of their reach.

'One stay here, one go in.' was the compromise reached after a lot of subdued chatter among them. So, before they knew what had happened, Moss sprinted for the river bank and plunged in.

They had swum in a restricted fashion in the giant Water Plants back in the forest, but this was a kind of freedom they had never even envisaged, and Moss took full advantage of the open water to show off his swimming abilities, diving beneath the surface to come up some distance away, causing a lot of concern among the females.

'You come back.' one of them screeched at Moss, who gave her his cheekiest grin and promptly dived under the surface. He broke water near the bank after some considerable time, and even Kel was getting worried for his safety.

Heaving himself out, Moss said as an aside to Kel, 'Now it's your turn, give 'em a fright if you can, it's the only way we can get our own back.'

The temptation to even the score was too much, and Kel leapt to his feet almost before Moss had finished speaking.

Eager hands made a grab for Kel, but he was too quick for them and made a dive for the water. The huge splash he made soaked those who had rushed to the bank to try and stop him, much to the amusement of the others.

He swam out, not as gracefully as Moss had, but considerably further, and that caused an outcry from the watching females. They seemed reluctant to enter the water, and shouted and leapt up and down on the river bank, obviously very angry, much to Moss's enjoyment.

A different cry suddenly went up, sheer terror in their combined voices, and Kel heard it. Instinctively he surged for the bank, arms and legs thrashing the water into a foaming mass as he accelerated forward. Eager hands grabbed him as he reached the bank, and only just in time as a pair of mighty jaws opened just behind him, to later shut with a deep thump.

The water monster, fully ten times the length of the onlookers, slid back into the deeper water, with only its stalk mounted eyes visible above the surface. It must have wondered how its prey had escaped.

'What was that thing?' exclaimed Kel, when he got his breath back.

'We call it Great Snapper,' one of the females said angrily, 'and you nearly got snapped by it. It swallow you in one piece, and you then no more.'

'Why didn't someone say that thing was in the water?' asked Moss, who was just as angry, but for a different reason.

'Not see very much, last time seen, very long ago. Sorry,' one of the females offered as some sort of possible apology.

The bathing party, having had enough excitement for one day, set off back to the collection of stone huts, several of them collecting fruits on the way.

'You eat all the fruits and pods of this forest?' asked Moss.

'Yes, all are good. The bad ones we dig up a long time ago. We not let them live here.' said one of the females, handing Moss a brightly coloured round fruit which he hadn't seen before.

'Eat, it very good.' and he did, and it was good. Kel was handed one of the new fruits, and having taken a small bite, due to his naturally suspicious nature of the unknown, he too consumed the rest of it.

The pair held their hands out for more, but were only given one more each. When they again tried to acquire more of the delicious fruit, heads were shaken, and one or two of the females looked rather sternly at their companions, who had provided the fruit in the first place.

Kel's suspicions were qualified when a little later, Moss began to giggle like a small boy, and he called out to him,

'You'd better try and sick that fruit up, it's not what you think.'

'Don't be silly, it's lovely, I'm lovely, they're all lovely.' responded a very jolly Moss.

Kel tried to be sick, but to no avail, the fruit was inside him and he was feeling all right so far.

'Funny lot, these females.' he muttered to himself, stumbling several times but helped up by his female companion who never left his side.

Silently the little troop made its way up the hill towards the encampment, except for the occasional giggle from Moss and the quiet muttering of endearments from Kel's companion.

Instead of going straight back to the main hut, which the pair expected, they were diverted off to one side and entered a smaller stone house on the outskirts of the group.

The whole party crowded in, and Moss and Kel were gently helped to lay down on a bed of soft fern like fronds.

By now the fruit had taken its full effect, and the two were in a state of euphoria, their eyes out of focus and their minds out of gear.

Moss began to make singing noises, but another mouth closed over his, and that was the end of the recital. Kel tried to sit up, but something soft and warm was holding him down and he soon gave up the unequal struggle and surrendered to the heady pheromone of the female's hair.

It was dark when they came to, Kel's little friend was still by his side, holding his hand and cooing softly.

'What happened?' asked Moss, the first to sit up, and trying to take stock of his surroundings.

'I think I'd rather not know.' replied Kel, knowing full well what had happened.

Moss was about to make a remark about his battered appendage when there was the sound of voices outside the hut. The Lesser Sun had risen and the soft silver light showed three older females entering the opening, and from the sound of their voices they were not in a happy mood.

One of them addressed Kel's companion in a stern voice,

'What you doing here?'

As she got no reply, she took the younger female by the arm and lifted her to her feet.

'You go out.' And she did, at full speed.

'What's been going on.' asked Moss, all innocence in his voice in case he too was going to be chastised.

'You not know?' asked one of the females, 'I am much surprised.' and she bent down to smell his breath.

'Not so surprised now. You feel good? You can walk?'

'I think so.' said Moss, staggering to his feet.

'Good, you come with us.' and Moss and Kel were led out of the hut, a little wobbly from their experience, but ambulant, with help.

It was only a short distance to the main hut they had found themselves in the night before, but to them it seemed a very long way indeed. Strong arms helped them along the way, but there was little of the jollity of the previous group of females who had taken them to the river.

The older female, who seemed to be in charge of the group, greeted them pleasantly enough, but she didn't smile, and when Moss did, she didn't return it.

A meal was presented and eaten, but in contrast to the previous night, there was very little conversation as there had been on the previous night.

Moss decided to try and get things going by asking if it would be all right for them to be on their way next day.

'Yes, but where will you go?' asked the older female.

'We have a Direction Pointer, and we follow wherever it points. We hope to discover many strange things to tell our Story Teller when we get back to our group in the forest.'

'Why you want to do this?' she asked.

Moss and Kel looked at each other for a suitable answer. They had both started on their journey because it was something exciting to do, and had never really thought about it any further.

'We just wanted to see what the rest of the world was like. According to the legends, it wasn't just the forest we lived in.' Moss didn't like the way the female had made their expedition seem of little value.

'Well, you can go next morning, but where will you go from here? There is only the plain you come in from and the valley forest below with the big water, and you not able to go through that.'

'Why not?' asked Kel.

'The big water go through big rocks, and no way up, no way around. We not go through, so you not go through.'

She seemed quite certain of that.

'We will have a look at that next day.' said Moss, trying to make his voice sound as positive as possible.

'We must have serviced just about every female in the group by now, so I wonder what they have in store for us tonight?' Moss quietly asked Kel when no one was looking.

'Perhaps it's just food time, and they want to be nice to us, but I doubt it. Watch out for those brightly coloured fruits we ate in their little forest, we don't want any more of those.'

They needn't have bothered. The juice from the fruits were already incorporated in the drink which was so liberally provided.

The Lesser Sun rose to bathe the area in its pale and gentle glow, lighting the way for the pair as they were hurried from hut to hut in a state of euphoric stupor. The females were making sure that at least some pregnances would be forthcoming, and if they didn't, it wouldn't be for the want of trying.

Five:
Two Kinds of Water

WHEN THEY AWOKE next day they were alone, except for the large female standing at the entrance to the hut.

'They've done it again,' Moss exclaimed, 'and I can't remember if I enjoyed it, and that's the annoying bit, apart from the soreness.'

'Me too. I won't be able to water in a straight line for days. They did what they thought they had to do in order to keep their group going, I suppose, but I wish we had had a little more say in the matter.'

Moss looked thoughtful for a moment or so, before saying,

'I haven't seen any males at all since we've been here, do you think there are any left? Maybe they only told us half the story of what happened.'

At this point the older female came in, looking in a much happier mood than the previous day, and actually smiling.

'You start your journey this day.' she said.

Not knowing if it was a question or a statement, Moss decided to take the initiative and said as firmly as he could, 'Yes, we do. We mustn't delay any longer, but we may come back this way on our return journey.'

The female couldn't hide her extreme pleasure at this news and the possibility of future romps, and smiled even wider.

'You eat, we take you to forest.' and with that she left.

A fresh platter of fruits and pods were produced, and the pair tucked in with gusto, later asking if they could take some of the food with them for their journey.

They checked their carry belts to make sure that nothing was missing, loaded up with food, and made sure their water bags were full. A feeling of relief and excitement gave an extra buoyancy to their steps as they set off for the forest, accompanied by a small group of females who were going to show them the barrier which had been mentioned earlier.

They were soon down by the water's edge, and followed a winding path along the smoothly flowing river until the trees began to thin out to low scrub, and the pathway came to an abrupt end.

Moss drew out his Greater Cutting Knife and cleared a new path for them, much to the amazement of the females who, by the look on their faces, had never seen such a knife before.

As the new pathway grew in length, Kel looked up from the task of pushing the cleared scrub to one side and exclaimed

'I see what the older female meant when she said we couldn't go past the forest. Look up there.'

Above them, the massive cliffs of a rift valley were closing in to a narrow vee shaped opening, the river speeding up as it threaded its way between the towering, almost vertical rock faces.

'We can't climb up there, but the water is getting through.' said Moss, pausing to survey the scene. 'Perhaps we could swim in the water and let it take us out to the other side.'

'What about the Water Snapper?' asked Kel, remembering his narrow escape. 'It may return, and there are no banks for us to climb up.'

A little more cutting and they had reached as far as they could go, the smooth black rock forming a barrier to their progress in the direction indicated by the Direction Pointer.

As they rested on the river bank, a large log floated by, and Moss had an idea.

'If we were to tie several of those logs together they should take our weight, and we could float down the waterway, and the Snapper wouldn't be able to reach us.'

Moss took charge and directed the females to collect the logs they would cut down from dead trees, and carry them to the waters edge.

Many admiring glances came their way as they swung the razor sharp blades, the trees crashing down one after another, to be cut into suitable lengths later.

Some vines were cut from a nearby clump, and the work of tying the logs into a platform began.

The Greater Sun had almost climbed to its midday height by the time the raft was completed, and was much larger than they had initially intended. They took a break to eat and drink, and then explained again to the females why they must go on with their journey.

It was plain to see that the females were disappointed at their imminent departure, but on mention of the fact that they may well return this way cheered them up a little, none of them realizing the impossibility of the two lads making their way upstream against the river flow.

It took all the available hands present to push the log raft to the waters edge, and then slide it down the bank and into the water. A vine had been attached to the raft to prevent it from floating away, and several eager hands held the floating log mass close to the bank in a last desperate hope that they wouldn't really go.

Moss and Kel jumped onto the raft, called for the vine to be released, and using the long steering poles they had thoughtfully cut, pushed the craft out into deeper water.

At the last possible moment, Kel's companion of yesterday ran forward and leapt across the intervening gap, landing safely on the raft.

'You can't come with us,' Moss shouted, struggling to hold the raft steady with his pole as the current took hold, 'you are only a female, and this is a man's journey.'

'I with you now. I no go back, I no swim.' she said smiling, and quickly untied one of the spare poles which had been tied down to the raft's surface in case of emergencies.

The departing cries of goodbye from the females on the bank soon faded as the trio poled the raft into the middle of the water flow, keeping it away from the rocky canyon walls which were looming up ahead.

'Now that you are with us, and we can't put you back on the bank, you must work as we do,' Moss said.

'I will, I will. I just as strong as you.' she replied, smiling.

'I'll bet she is,' thought Kel, 'and just as smart, I wouldn't wonder.'

As they entered the gap between the towering cliffs, the raft gathered speed as the waterway narrowed, and they had their work cut out trying to keep it in the middle of the flow.

Several times the raft drifted towards the sharp rocky edge of the gorge as the river turned and twisted its way through, and the female proved her worth as she bent to the pole and helped keep the raft on course.

The Greater Sun began its long drift down towards the horizon, and the light was lessening a little as the team frantically poled their raft around yet another tortuous bend in the now darkening canyon.

As they cleared the bend, the river opened out to nearly twice its normal width, and the flow slowed down accordingly. Ahead was a small beach of sand, and they poled their way towards it, longing to take a much needed rest from their exertions.

The raft ground to a halt against the gently sloping bank of sand, and Kel jumped ashore to secure the vine to a nearby rock. If the raft drifted off now, they would be trapped here forever, as the cliffs above them were just as steep as those at the beginning of their journey through the gorge.

'We may as well stay here for the night.' Moss said, as he sat down on the soft sandy bank. 'I doubt we'll find a better place.'

The food supplies were brought out, and they had their evening meal as the last rays of the Greater Sun lit up the sky in streaks of yellow and red, heralding a good day on the morrow.

'We don't know your name.' said Kel, turning to their female companion.

'I'm called Jaylec,' she responded with her usual smile, 'but I like Jay better. You call me Jay.'

With little else to do, after they had made sure that the raft was still securely tied to the rock, they prepared to settle down for the night, Moss volunteering to take the first watch.

Kel scooped out a depression in the soft sand and settled himself into it, curling up for sleep, but hardly had he closed his eyes when he felt another little body cuddle into his back, an arm slide around his chest, and he was held captive by his admirer.

During the night, something large and sounding very angry thrashed about in the deep water just off shore, and Moss was thankful they hadn't encountered it while they were afloat.

While they were changing over shifts, a small shower of rocks crashed down from high up on the cliff face, fortunately missing them and landing in the water downstream.

'Not so safe as it looks,' commented Moss as he lay down to sleep, 'I wonder what caused that?'

Kel had no answer, so didn't say anything as he strained his eyes in the pale light of the Lesser Sun, looking for movement high up in the rocks.

Nothing further disturbed the travellers during the night, except the odd dream, one of which brought Moss out of his sleep and bounding to his feet before he knew what he had done. After a quick snack and a chuckle about the incident, he was peacefully back in his slumbers.

The Greater Sun broke the horizon in a blaze of glory, lighting up the little wavelets on the river with tips of fire.

The crew were already up, gathering their belongings and preparing to set out for the day's journey downstream.

A shadow passed overhead, momentarily blocking out the light from the rising sun, and they had a quick glimpse of something very large on leathery wings and equipped with a wicked set of taloned feet, glide down the rift between the cliffs and out of sight around the next bend. Seconds later, there was an agonizing scream which turned their blood to ice water. Something had been caught for breakfast, and was complaining bitterly about it.

They looked at each other in dismay.

'So far we haven't seen anything like that, and I hoped we wouldn't. We've only seen them in the forest back home, and that wasn't very often, so we'll have to be on the lookout for the Leather Wings, although there isn't much we can do about it when we do see them, except hide.' Moss anxiously looked up, but the sky was clear except for the rising sun.

The raft was pushed out into deeper water, and Kel took a running jump to get on board as it left the sandy beach behind. They poled it out some way, but not into the middle of the river as they had done the day before in case they had to make a dash for the shore, not that there was much shore ahead, just sheer rocks, but it felt better that way.

By using a pole as a depth gauge, they were able to keep in relatively shallow waters, hoping that the giant Water Snapper would be unable to follow them, but it was only a hope, not knowing how far inshore the creature could go.

They passed through another very narrow section of the gorge, the water flow speeded up considerably, and nearly wrecked the raft on a rocky projection which they hadn't seen until too late.

It ripped out two of the logs on one end, and Jay lay full length holding on to the loosened logs until they reached calmer waters and were able to retie them into place with some spare vines they had thoughtful enough to bring.

The water flow was now almost non-existent, so wide was the river at this point, and they had to use the poles to get any noticeable movement at all, and that meant keeping as near inshore as possible.

It was during this muscle aching exercise, poling the raft along, that they noticed high up on the cliff, small figures running about on some ledges. The occasional dark hole indicated that a cave of some sort was present in the cliff face, and was probably the home of the cliff runners.

All was well until a small shower of stones fell around them, and realizing the height from which they had come, and the force with which they would strike, Moss immediately gave orders to pole out a little further, so getting out of range of the stone throwers.

This wasn't as easily done as said, because the river was quite deep a short way out, and the poles failed to reach the bottom.

Kel cupped his hands around his mouth and shouted up to the cliff runners, asking them to stop, but they didn't, replying in strange words which none of them understood.

'Nothing for it, just try to dodge them when you see them coming.' was all Moss could offer as a defence against the onslaught.

They were lucky, and no one was hit by the stones, although several landed harmlessly on the actual raft.

Soon they were past the point where the ledges ran, and the throwers couldn't go any further. The trio on the raft jumped up and down, making faces at the cliff runners and laughing as loudly as possible.

'Hope we don't have to pass this way again, or if we do, they have a very short memory.' Kel said, a touch of joviality in his voice for the first time since they had left the sandy beach. 'I wonder why they were so aggressive?'

'Looking back at the cliff, I would think that they are trapped there, as I can't see any way up to the top or down to the water. Food and water must be a bit of a problem for them, and I don't suppose they are very happy about that.' Moss offered as an explanation.

The midday meal was taken as they poled their way along, and by mid afternoon it was evident that the river was going to narrow down again. The current became turbulent, and the rocky cliffs closed in like two giant shields to shut off some of the light from the Greater Sun, making it a gloomy part of the journey.

Moss was looking for a safe place to stop for a break in their journey when they rounded a bend and were confronted by a sheer rock wall.

The river seemed to enter a large opening in the rock face, and before they could do anything about it, the raft picked up speed and was on its way towards the hole.

'Get down flat and hold onto anything you can.' yelled Kel, throwing himself down. 'There's nothing we can do about it, just hold onto the bindings and hope the river goes straight through whatever this place is.'

The raft was fairly racing along now, luckily in the middle of the river, and as they entered the vast hole in the cliff the light suddenly went, and they were alone in the darkness with only the sound of the water rushing along beneath.

Several times the raft hit the side of the tunnel as it careered along, nearly spilling its human cargo overboard, but they managed to hang onto the binding vines as the craft twisted and turned in the turbulence.

As the noise of the rushing water subsided a little, and the raft ceased to bob about quite so much, Kel shouted out,

'Are you two still there?'

'Only just.' the deeper voice of Moss replied.

'Me here too.' but it was tinged with fear.

'I think we're almost out of the hole, I can see some light ahead.' called Kel, but he was mistaken.

The light was coming from something growing on the walls of the huge tunnel, and hanging down from the roof and walls were a countless number of thread like tendrils, some reaching the level of the water.

'Oh no,' exclaimed Moss, who had risen to his knees, 'over the side and hang on, they look like Whip Vines'.

All three slipped over the edge of the now slowly moving raft just in time, as the first of the vines brushed across the logs. There were several jerks as the vines having contacted something, and not knowing any better, tried to grab the raft as a possible source of food.

A sudden scream from Moss indicated that something had touched him.

'Are you all right Moss?' Kel managed to gargle, spitting out a mouthful of water at the same time.

'Yes, I think so. A vine just touched my head, grabbed some hair and pulled it out by the roots, it hurts, but not too much damage so far. Keep as low in the water as possible.'

The raft drifted on, and the unhappy and very frightened three clung on tightly to the binding vines around its side, keeping themselves as low in the water as possible, yet in fear of being attacked by whatever might be swimming around beneath them.

The light in the tunnel slowly dimmed as the strange growth on its walls diminished, leaving the trio in total darkness again.

'I've managed to get a stave free,' called Kel, 'and if I hold it up and nothing grabs it, I think it should be safe to climb onto the raft again, as we are at great risk of being attacked by whatever might be in the water.'

Kel held the stave up as high as he could, but nothing tried to take it away from him, the only sound now being the quiet swish of the water under the raft, and then a scraping noise as the stave touched a lower section of the tunnel roof as the raft drifted on.

'Get back onto the logs, I think we are getting too close to the tunnel wall, and we could get scraped off.' Kel was already halfway back onboard.

They huddled together in the middle of the floating collection of logs, holding on to the binding vines in case anything tried to snatch them off in the darkness, and not knowing where they were going.

A faint glimmer of light up ahead gave them a little hope as the craft gathered speed in a narrow section of the dark tunnel, and suddenly they were out in the sunlight, covering their eyes against the brilliant glare.

Three simultaneous sighs of relief sounded out as they realized they had survived the dangers and traumas of the tunnel, and apart from being very wet, were all in one piece, except for Moss, who had a small section of his head hair missing.

The river had slowed down a little and thankfully widened out again, the cliffs had receded back from the banks leaving an apparently normal river bank covered in short foliage interspersed with the occasional clump of rocks.

'We must dry everything out while we have the chance.' said Moss, who had already divested himself of his carry belt and its hanging equipment.

The first thing Kel checked was their store of dried berries.

'It's a good thing the draw string on the bag of dried black berries Mec gave us held the water out, or it could have expanded to enormous proportions by now, and we would have lost our emergency food supplies.' Kel was inspecting all the little bags containing their survival equipment, and making sure the contents were dry.

The further the raft drifted down stream, the wider the river became and the more they had to use the poles to make any headway. The cliffs were now receding to become a low ridge, a long way back from the river bank.

A few trees, interspersed with bushes, began to appear as the raft slowly glided on, but nothing like those they were used to in the main forest.

While Jay kept the raft on course with her pole, Moss and Kel readjusted the vine bindings, replacing some which had been damaged when the raft rubbed against the cliff and the tunnel walls.

They decided to pull into the shore, take a rest, and see what the land was like. Their food stocks were going down steadily and needed to be replaced in case there wasn't the chance to do so later.

As the raft drew nearer to the bank, Jay, who was kneeling on the edge of the logs, called the others over,

'Look at this.' she said, pointing to a mass of white waving strands in the water below.

'Is it a kind of grass?' she asked.

Moss lowered his pole to try and entwine a few of the waving strands, but they immediately retracted back into the soft mud, and out of sight.

'It's a life form of some sort, but I've never seen anything quite like it before. Mec said we would find all sorts of strange things on our journey, and it seems he was right, as always.'

'They look harmless enough.' Kel said as he made the raft fast to a convenient bush with the mooring vine.

The white tendrils retreated into the mud to avoid Kel's feet as he stepped ashore.

For a long time they talked over the high points of their adventure on the raft, while sitting on the river bank, and then just looked at the view of the river as it spilled out onto the broad flood plain.

Their reverie was disturbed by a grunting noise, and they sprang to their feet, Moss with his bladed stave at the ready.

Peering out from the bushes was a large fat creature on four legs with a long snout waving about in the air as if it was sniffing out some delicious smell. It didn't seem frightened of them, moving a little closer and then sniffing the air again.

Before they could stop her, Jay had moved forward and reached out to touch the long snout of the creature, which was still waving about. There was little reaction to her contact, except for the long thin snout curling around her hand for a moment, and then letting it go. It repeated this action several times, and then moved forward to almost brush up against Jay, who seemed to show no fear whatsoever.

'That was a dangerous thing to do,' commented Moss, his stave at the ready, 'it may have thought you were a meal on legs, and there would have been little we could do about it, considering its size.'

'I just knew it safe,' Jay replied, 'I always know.'

'That's a useful thing to be able to do.' Kel said, realizing the possible future benefits of such a skill.

'Yes,' Moss replied, 'and you can only make one mistake.'

The fat grey creature had now stripped a bunch of leaves off a nearby bush with its nose, and turning to Jay, seemed to be offering them to her.

As her hand took hold of the leaves, the snout let go, swung around to strip off some more leaves, and then stuffed them into its mouth.

'Pity you aren't a leaf eater, you wouldn't have to work very hard to get your food with one of those around.' Kel said with a laugh, and the whole atmosphere on the river bank changed to one of peace and friendliness.

Somehow the creature engendered a feeling of well-being among the trio, and they relaxed to lay down on the short grass, and give their tired muscles a rest before continuing their journey.

Moss woke up from a long doze, and realized that Kel was missing, although Jay was still lying on the bank, fast asleep.

He was about to call out his name, when Kel came pushing through the bushes, his arms laden with fruits and pods.

'You should have told me what you were about to do.' chided Moss, trying to look cross, but failing, due to his relief upon Kel's return.

'You were asleep, and I thought you might need the rest, anyway, our grey friend followed me, keeping quite close at all times, so I don't think anything else would have stood much of a chance.'

As the light had dimmed a little, it was decided that they would stay on the river bank for the night, and resume their travelling next day, there being little point in going on now as they wouldn't get very far before it was dark, and finding another safe place in time couldn't be guaranteed.

What did surprise them as they settled down for the night, was the grey creature which had befriended them, also curled up as close as it could. It showed no fear at all, but made snoring noises until Jay got up and stretched the snout out into a straight line, and then they all slept peacefully until the dawn broke.

Moss was the first to awake, yawn, stretch, and then notice that their grey friend of yesterday had gone. Jay seemed saddened at its departure, but soon cheered up when they prepared the raft for the next leg of their journey.

They hadn't been afloat for long when the raft ground to a halt on a mud bank just below the surface, and it took a lot of heavy poling to get it off and into deeper water.

The further downstream they went, the further out into the river they had to go to get water deep enough to float the raft, until the shoreline was only just visible as a hazy smudge on their left, and nothing but open water on the other side.

'I don't like the idea of being so far from land.' Moss said, as he pushed on the pole to try and increase the speed of the sluggish raft.

'If anything happens out here we won't stand a chance of getting back to solid ground before it's too late, that's if we can get there at all.'

'What do you suggest then?' Asked Kel.

Before he could answer, Jay had gone to the edge of the raft to check on the water depth with a stave, and gave a little cry of surprise as her foot went straight through the surface of one of the logs to reveal a seething mass of chewed up wood and a large number of the white worms.

She pulled her foot out quickly, scraped off several squashed worms and put her foot over the side to wash off the remaining mess.

Moss and Kel rushed over to see what the trouble was, and stared in horror as they realized just what had happened.

'It must be those white thread like worm things' said Moss. 'When we stopped on the bank for a rest, they must have sensed the logs above them, cut their way in and have been chewing away ever since.'

'We'll have to make it to the shore now, we have no alternative, the whole lot may fall apart at any time, and then we'll be in deep trouble.'

They spread their weight as evenly as possible on the logs, ever fearful of a foot disappearing into a mass of sticky white worms, or even worse, going right through the weakened logs into the water beneath.

They poled on, not really sure they were still going down because it was so spread out now and the water seemed to be almost still. Kel noticed that the logs were now flexing in rhythm to the small waves which had become apparent of late, and he thought about tightening the vines.

'The whole structure has weakened almost to breaking point,' Kel said, 'and we'd better get to the bank soon, I don't think it can last much longer without retying it all.'

'I agree, but how?' Moss didn't have any ideas either.

They pressed on, steering the raft towards the distant bank as far as the mud banks would allow, but getting no closer as far as they could tell.

A deep resounding boom echoed across the water, and they all turned to see what could have caused it. In the far distance, almost on the horizon, a plume of smoke sped skywards, lightning flickering around its crown as it reached a few fleecy clouds in the higher atmosphere.

'What was that?' they chorused almost together.

No one had an answer, but along with the smoke, streaks of fire were now leaping skywards.

It was Moss who spotted the next event which was to threaten their survival. Speeding across the relative calm waters towards them was a huge tidal wave.

'If that hits us we are done for!' Moss cried out in sheer panic, 'our only hope is to hang onto the vines as tightly as possible, and hope we get washed ashore.'

The eerie silence was broken at last as the speeding wave drew ever closer.

A rustling, rushing noise grew in volume until it became a dull roar, and the wave was upon them. Many times their height, it lifted the wobbly raft high up, so that they could see the land clearly, and then it carried them forward at an ever increasing pace, as the wave reached the shallows and speeded up.

It seemed to take forever, the journey across the shallows, and then they saw the river bank racing towards them.

'Hold on tight, I think the logs are breaking up.' Kel needn't have said anything, their fingers had almost melded with the holding vines, as their white knuckles showed.

There was a sudden upsurge as the wave hit the bank, throwing the raft up into the air, to crash down a few seconds later in a mass of spray.

Several of the logs on the outer edge of the raft had broken away, the holding vines whipping about like living creatures as the stress was relieved.

The power of the wave lessened as it raced inland, lowering the remains of the frail raft and its hapless occupants from its lofty crest almost down to the level of the ground, until it finally spent itself in a mass of frothing water and mud, the raft breaking up into a shattered heap of chewed timber and squirming white worms.

After getting back on their feet as the spent wave retreated, the three looked at each other in sheer disbelief, and then, covered in mud and pulped wood from the remains of the shattered raft, hugged each other in turn, tears of relief running down their faces.

When they had got their breath back, Moss set about trying to rescue the remains of the larger logs, as their staves and spare vine ropes were attached to them.

Kel and Jay unlashed the equipment as Moss dragged the logs in, and before long, as dirty as they were, some sort of jollity had returned to the party.

'Where do we go from here?' asked Moss, looking around to find something different to water and the unending grassy plain.

'I can only suggest we use the Direction Pointer, and follow its indicated course as we have done before.' Kel answered, 'I for one would like to wash off this mud, it stinks, so let's hope we find clean water before too long. I don't want to go near that river again, anyway, the water will be muddy for some time, after that upheaval.'

They set up the indicator, picked up their possessions and trudged off in the direction it had shown them, three very grubby, hot and tired individuals, but happy to be alive.

Moss remarked that they seemed to be going away from the river, and put it down to the fact that the river had gradually turned away from their intended heading earlier on, and they hadn't noticed.

The first of a small group of rocks could be seen just ahead of them, and they diverted off their intended course out of sheer curiosity.

As they drew nearer, it was obvious that the group of rocks was much bigger than they had first thought, and were unlike any others they had come across so far. Almost black in colour and sponge-like in texture, they were very hard. Climbing up the pile to get a better view of the surrounding countryside, Moss suddenly called out in surprise.

'Be careful as you come up, the rocks are very sharp, but you must come and look at this.'

After struggling up to the top of the rock pile, the others joined him and they looked down into a large deep pool of crystal clear water.

'First, we must make sure something nasty hasn't made its home here, and then we can fill up our water bags with clean water instead of the dirty looking stuff we got from the river. After that, if it's still safe, we can wash off this stinking mud from ourselves and the equipment.'

Moss attached the largest fruit they had with them to a long length of vine, and dangled it into the water. As nothing much happened, except that the fruit looked a lot cleaner after its dunking, he tied the vine to the end of his stave and swung it out over the middle of the pool until the fruit was hardly visible as it sank into the depths. Still no reaction of any sort, so Moss deemed it safe to lower one of them to the water level, and fill up their water bags, after first washing them out well.

With as much fresh water stored as the containers would hold, and their own thirst slaked, Moss decided it was time to take a bath, one at a time just in case something unexpected happened.

Kel was the first to be lowered down with the aid of a vine rope, and plunged into the cool clear water. He was quite a good swimmer, and showed off appallingly by diving deep, and then surging up to the surface to rise some distance out of the water before crashing back, causing wavelets to lap around the rim of the pool.

Jay was quite impressed at his prowess in the water and he would have gone on, going deeper and deeper if Moss hadn't called him out.

As Kel reached the rim of the water hole, Moss, not to be outdone, took a short run of three steps and launched himself in a flying leap towards the centre of the pool, to disappear into its depths for several seconds. Kel was a little worried as the time went by, and then Moss surfaced to leap out of the water even higher than Kel had.

When Moss finally got out of the pool, it was Jay's turn, but she wasn't as used to the water as the other two, although she had lived by the river.

She carefully climbed down with the aid of the vine rope, and lowered herself into the water, keeping near the edge of the rocks. It was this cautious approach to the water which largely saved her life.

Suddenly the centre of the pool erupted in a fountain of foam and a large grey-brown shape reared up to look around for the thing which had dared to disturb it.

Jay was only a short distance from the rocky edge when the monster appeared, and her arms cleaved the water in a frantic effort to reach the safety of the rim. Moss had grabbed his stave and was about to throw it when he realized it would be of little use against such a large creature, and might even make it more angry. They could only stand there and watch as Jay struggled to reach safety, the whole scene happening in apparent slow motion, and the water creature gaining every second.

As Jay reached the rim of the water hole and began to climb out, a clawed arm raked the rock beside her, leaving deep scratch marks in the hard stone.

Moss and Kel had found some loose stones, and began to rain them down onto the creature, diverting its attention for a few moments and so allowing Jay to climb out of its reach.

Panting for breath, she joined them on the top of the rock pile, well out of reach of the water monster who was churning up the water in a frenzied fit of rage as its intended meal had escaped.

'It must live deep down in the pool, well out of our sight, waiting for something to come here for a drink, and then snap. Nasty.' Moss pulled a face of disgust to reinforce his opinion of the creature.

'I'm not so sure,' said Kel, 'we had a difficult time climbing up here, so I don't see how any of the creatures we have seen so far could do better, or even as well.'

'It must get its food from somewhere, and a lot of it, just look at its size.' Moss didn't like to make a statement, and not be able to back it up.

They climbed down the rocks to the plain below, and were soon on their way again, only to come across another group of similar rocks with a pool, and then Moss expounded on his theory.

'I think these pools are linked together underground, and the creature can swim between them when it needs to, that's why we could use the water for so long before it appeared, as it was probably some distance away and heard us through the water as we splashed about.'

As Kel couldn't refute this argument, and wasn't too keen to disprove the theory by tempting the water monster to emerge from the second pool, he just agreed with Moss and promptly changed the subject.

'It looks as if there's something on the horizon, a high ridge or maybe another cliff like the one we saw when we were with Jay's people.'

There was something, but it only showed as a faint smudge, a mere difference in visual texture to that which surrounded them.

The little troop marched on, passing several other outcrops of volcanic rock, which inspired Moss to expound on his theory of the underground tunnels linking them, and the water monsters ability to travel between the outcrops.

As they travelled on, the terrain began to change again, shallow valleys nestling between slight rises in the ground produced a plentiful supply of recognizable fruits and pods, so there was little difficulty in feeding themselves.

The precious supply of dried berries which Mec had provided were still almost intact.

The further they travelled, the more pronounced the hills and valleys became, and on the sixth day since leaving the river they saw the sea for the first time in their lives.

They had camped on the top of a particularly steep hill, finding a cosy opening in a rock formation which was easily guarded, but as the light had diminished somewhat upon arriving, they hadn't noticed the full significance of what could be seen from their high vantage point.

The next morning was a different story, the mists of the night rolled away, showing a long sloping plain leading down to a vast stretch of water, still greyish in the early morning light.

Jay was the first one to see it, as the others were still busy gathering their equipment together, ready for the next stage of their march.

'Come and look!' she called, 'a great water has gone over all the land for as far as I see.'

The other two rushed up to the vantage point, and were stunned by what they saw.

'I know the river spilled out over a great space, but that is even bigger,' Kel said. 'and if it's in our way, how can we cross it? It might go on for ever and ever.'

'One good thing about it, we shan't go short of drinking water.' Moss added, trying not to look as overwhelmed at the sight of it as he felt.

It took two more days to reach the sea, and that surprised them all as it didn't look that far from the hilltop.

But they were in for another surprise on the way, as they came upon their first encounter with a relic from the time of the giants other than the remains of the concrete building in the forest.

They had just panted their way up a grassy slope, and as they paused for a rest at the top, Moss pointed out the light reflecting from what he thought was a pool of water.

'I don't think it's water.' Kel remarked, not sure what it was. 'It's too shiny for that, let's go and see what it is.'

They almost ran down the hill, not just because it was so steep, but because curiosity had got the better of them yet again.

Moss, being the one with the longer legs, arrived at the half buried stainless steel silo first, and stood in amazement at the tall shiny structure.

Raising his arm, he hit the smooth surface with his clenched fist, and jumped back startled at the dull hollow boom which followed.

'What is it, and what is it made of? I've never seen anything like this before.'

'I have.' Jay joined in, 'The hairless man who wanted our men to go into the forbidden lands had little pieces of shiny stuff like that, he called it meetel, I think. He said it was good, and he would give our men lots of good things if they get little bits of it for him.

'When they come back, they get ill, and some go to the sky, and all lose their hair and look ugly.

'Now they all gone, only females left. They leave the shiny bits in a hutt outside our group, but no one go there, and the hairless man not come back to take the shiny bits'.

Moss stood back from the silo, deep in thought, and said,

'Somehow I don't think it's the meetel which causes the illness, because plants are growing all around this huge piece of it, and they are no different than those over there.' he said, pointing up the long slope, 'So it must be something else in the area where the little pieces of meetel are found which is so bad.'

Moss dug about in one of his equipment bags, and withdrew a small flint blade.

'Let's see if we can cut a little piece of this meetel off, it may be useful at some time.' and with that he ran the blade across the surface of the silo. The screech of flint on hardened alloyed chrome steel made them all jump back, as though the silo had spoken to them.

'It hardly left a scratch,' remarked Kel, going up to the silo when his fear had subsided a little, 'if we could get little pieces of this strange stuff, we could make some very good Cutting Knives from it.'

'Perhaps that was why the hairless man wanted it, so there must be some way of making knives from the meetel pieces.' Moss was quick to see the possibilities of such a material.

Try as they might, they were unable to obtain the metal they wanted, and eventually gave up the idea, Moss saying that they should keep an eye out for any little bits that might be lying around as they journeyed on.

'As we are near the water, let's fill up our water bags.' Kel suggested, all agreed, and they set off for the beach.

On the way, they passed several stumpy remains of old buildings, only a small section of them still showing above ground as over the years, wind drift and the usual upheavals of nature had buried most of them from sight.

The soft golden sands of the beach stretched out for some considerable distance before they came to the water, and they approached it warily as they hadn't seen waves of such a size before.

Moss was first into the water, and having gone in up to his knees, cupped his hands to scope up some water to drink.

'Don't drink this water!' he exclaimed in disgust, spitting it out and rubbing his mouth. 'it's bad, and tastes awful, even worse than the river water after the floater broke up.'

'Quick, come back to the sand! There's something coming towards you and moving very fast.' Kel screamed.

Moss needed no second warning, he turned and rapidly splashed his way back to the others just in time as the expected set of jaws snapped behind him, the creature thrashing about in the shallow water in frustration.

'You really must be more careful,' Kel chided, not wishing to lose his friend, 'any new thing we come across should be studied first for possible dangers.'

The trio sat down on the soft sand, wondering why the plentiful supply of water was so bad to the taste, and more to the point, how they were going to cross it, as the Direction Pointer indicated that they should go straight out to sea.

'We can't make a floating log bot, or whatever the giants called it, as there are no trees near here.

'Swimming would only provide food for the monsters which are no doubt out there, and if they didn't get us, we couldn't possibly swim such a great distance anyway.'

Kel had stated the obvious, which the others were thinking, and they had to agree with him.

'The land curves away on both sides of us in the opposite direction to which we should go, so what shall we do?' asked Moss, not really expecting an answer to the problem, as he had none either.

'Do you think it would be worth while climbing that hill over there to see if the land does curve back towards the water again? And if it does, we would at least be going in the right direction.' said Kel.

'We can do that, but I don't think it will get us much closer really. We need to go over the water, but without something to float on it, we can't, so we must find something.' Moss made it sound like an order rather than an opinion. All three turned away from the water, with little hope in their hearts.

They trudged back up the sandy beach with little enthusiasm, as their goal seemed to be blocked for the time being by the massive extent of the ocean, and they had little hope of finding anything which would float.

After a long walk they reached the top of the hill, climbed the rocky outcrop which crowned it and had their worst fears confirmed. They had been on the end of a peninsula which had reached out some considerable distance into the ocean, and the land curved back from it in both directions for as far as they could see.

'We shall have to find some means of making a Floater of some description if we want to carry on in the direction indicated.' Moss mumbled, almost to himself, but the others heard it and felt the same dismay as he did.

'It looks as if there are some more remains of the giant's work over there.' Kel pointed to a collection of rocky stumps which protruded from the otherwise smooth undulating downland which lay between them and the beach.

'Well it's worth a look at, there's nothing much for us up here and who knows what we might find.' Moss seemed to have brightened up a little, having something positive to do.

The stubby remains of the old farm complex was far bigger than it had appeared from the hilltop, and the trio were soon lost in a labyrinth of decaying concrete walls, which to them seemed massive.

'The giants must have been very big indeed if these are the remains of their hutts.' Kel commented, standing on one of the walls and surveying the outline of the building.

Later, a piece of glass caused a great deal of excitement, as they had seen nothing like it before.

'It looks like the hard water which used to sometimes fall from the sky,' Kel remarked, 'except that was always round, and this is flat, and it isn't cold like the hard water was.'

'It must be something the giants have made,' Moss added, 'let's see if there's any more.'

They spent some time looking for more glass, but found none, but Jay stubbed her toe on the slightly protruding end of a buried stainless steel feeding trough, and that more than made up for the lack of glass.

They dug the end of the trough free from the ground which had imprisoned it for so long with the aid of their staves, using the blunt end rather than risk breaking the precious cutting blades. It was only when the entire end of the trough was made visible that Moss gave a cry of excitement and said, 'If the other end is like this, we may have our bot.'

All three dug with renewed vigour as they now had a real purpose in mind, and the trough slowly came to light.

'Do you think it a giant's bot?' asked Jay, panting a little from the exertion.

'I don't know, we may have a better idea when we have all of it revealed.' answered Moss, now a quarter the way along its length, although he didn't know it.

As the light began to fade, they called a halt to the digging operation, deciding that a good rest was called for as there was little need to rush the excavation. The next day would reveal the trough, or so they hoped.

During the meal, Moss outlined his plan for using the trough as a floating carrier to take them over the sea, but the one thing they couldn't resolve was the means of propelling it.

The idea of using their hands as paddles was put forward, but was soon dropped as it could have meant having them bitten off by what ever took a fancy to them as a tasty morsel, and they had no doubts there would be lots of takers for that option.

Moss knew what he wanted, a flat piece of material to put on the end of the staves to act as a paddle, but there wasn't anything around which would serve that purpose.

Despite the fact that they hadn't found a means of propelling the boat they were so sure of recovering from the ground, they found it difficult to sleep that night as the excitement level grew the more they talked about the forthcoming journey over the water.

Early daylight saw them up and about, fed, watered and ready to continue the digging, and although it was quite cool in the early morning light, they were soon sweating profusely as the earth flew in all directions from their stabbing staves, and more of the feeding trough came to light.

By midday the whole trough was exposed, and they had managed to drag it clear of its burial site.

'How do you know it will float?' asked Kel, 'It's nothing like the tree trunks we used before.'

'I don't really know, I just think it will somehow. Anyway, we can try it out a soon as we get it down to the water, and if it doesn't, we have only lost some time and a little work.'

It took them two days and a lot more even harder work to drag and lever the cumbersome feeding trough down to the distant beach.

Having got it there, they suddenly realized that they would have to go into the water in order to get it afloat, and the possibility of being attacked by the denizens of the deep precluded that action.

'Now what we do?' It was Jay's turn to show her frustration at the turn of events.

As there was no answer forthcoming, they all retired to their little encampment at the top end of the beach, sat down, and generally felt and looked miserable.

Again it was Moss who saved the day.

'I've noticed that the water goes up and down the beach every day, so if we wait until it has gone down as far as it can, and drag the bot after it, we can get in and if the end in the water floats, as I think it will, we shall be able to float away as the water returns up the beach.

'If it doesn't float, then we can get out of it from the end which is still on the sand, and no harm is done.'

'That still leaves the problem of making it go where we want it to.' Kel said. 'And we will still have to collect a lot of fruit to eat on the way, as we have no idea how long the journey will take.'

'We will find a way, sooner or later.' said Moss, sounding a lot more confident than he actually felt.

The following day they set about working out a stratagem for completing all their needs for the journey across the sea.

Food wasn't too much of a problem, as they could go back to where they had seen plenty of fruit, but how much to take with them was another matter, as it could well get over ripe and rot before they had eaten it.

The water supply was restricted to the amount that they could carry in their water bags, and as Jay didn't have one, it meant that they would have to share their supply with her.

All the other bags in which they carried their equipment could be emptied and filled with water, so increasing their supply a little, but it was their main concern that they couldn't carry enough for their needs having no idea of how long the journey would take. Jay suggested that they could catch rain water, but they weren't sure if it rained in this part of the world.

The lack of a means to make paddles was the only problem which had them beaten, but Moss wouldn't give up on the idea, and spent most of his time wandering around the old buildings, looking for anything which might be of use.

The food gathering expedition, when it finally got under way, proved to be most productive, as Jay found a small tree which she recognized as similar to those she had used before, and it provided them with long creeper like strands from which she was able to make carrying bags for the fruit. This enabled them to carry much more in the way of provisions than they had anticipated, and releasing other bags to hold extra water.

The problem of the flat material for the paddles was partly resolved by Moss, insofar that he had found some thin whip like growths from which he wove paddle like blades, weaving stout bladed grasses in between the frame strands to fill in the gaps.

The paddle blades were then attached to staves, and leaning over a rock so he could reach the water, he practised 'paddling' as best he could, and thought that if they made some spares in case they were affected by the water after prolonged use, they should be able to move the 'bot' without too much difficulty.

With all possible water bags full and safely tied off, woven bags of fruit and pods piled in a heap, some not quite ripe at Kel's suggestion, the staves and coils of vine lashed together and the feeding trough tied to a nearby rock, the trio were ready to try their luck on the ocean.

When the tide was nearly at full ebb, they moved their supplies down the beach in stages so that when boarding, they wouldn't have too far to transport their possessions.

The feeding trough was dragged down at the last moment, and as the tide turned, they piled everything into the 'Bot', climbed in themselves, and waited for the rising tide to lift them clear. Slowly the water crept up the beach, and before long the front end of the trough began to rise and fall rhythmically with the incoming waves.

The occasional larger wave swept in with great force, and the whole trough heaved itself high up into the air, returning to the sand with a resounding thud, while the occupants clung on for dear life.

By the time the water had reached the rear end of the trough, the rocking motion for those on board was becoming a little too much.

'I hope it's not like this when we reach the open water.' Jay said, looking wistfully towards the top end of the beach and the hills beyond.

'It shouldn't be this bad, I think it's the slope of the beach which makes the waves so big.' Moss added, trying to add a word of comfort to the rather doubtful start of their adventure. After several more bone jarring thumps on the beach as the larger waves raced in, Kel had had enough and suggested, 'if we push with the staves when the next big wave comes in, we should be able to move it out into deeper water. All that's happening now is that we are being pushed back up the beach each time a big wave hits us.'

They unleashed three staves, and stood by ready for the next upsurge. As the trough reared up, they drove the staves into the sand and pushed with all their might, the rear end came free, and they were on their way.

'Quick, work with the paddles.' called Moss, who had already grabbed his and was frantically driving it into the water as though his life depended on it.

With three paddles thrashing the water, the trough slowly headed out to sea, the height of the waves diminished giving way to a gentle swell. Gradually the frantic paddling gave way to a more rhythmic action, and the trough steadily glided ahead, while the land slowly disappeared from view.

When the Greater Sun had reached its zenith, Moss called a halt to the paddling and suggested they rest and eat.

Tired and sore muscles sagged with relief as they sat down in the bottom of the trough and relaxed.

'What happens if we run out of food and water before we find the other land?' asked Jay a little hesitatingly, as she didn't want to put a damper on the otherwise successful beginning of their trip.

'I've thought of that,' said Moss, 'when the water supply is half used up, and if there is no rain for us to catch, then we use the Direction Pointer to guide us back to the beach. I know we'll be back where we started, but at least we'll be alive and can try again further along.'

They took up the paddles again, and despite their tired muscles, drove the trough forward with the enthusiasm only found among those who didn't realize how the odds were stacked against them, or didn't care.

All was going well until Jay gave a little scream. Something had snatched the paddle blade from the end of her stave. Fortunately she managed to hold onto the precious stave itself, but the look of fear on her face only served to reinforce the new problem they were now going to be faced with.

Only a limited number of spare paddles were available, and no material to replace them with, and this clearly worried the otherwise unshakeable Moss.

'From now on, we will only use two paddles at a time, one on each side of the bot. As we put them into the water, we must look out for anything which might try to take them, and withdraw them at once if we see anything.'

'What if the creature stays around waiting for us to offer the paddle again?' asked Kel, always ready with another question.

'Then we'll stab it with a bladed stave, the non paddler can have that job.' Moss replied, hoping against hope that it would not come to that.

By the time that the Greater Sun had sunk to the horizon, lighting the sky up in a brilliant display of red and yellow streaks, the crew were well and truly spent.

It was decided to take as long a rest as they thought they needed, sleeping in the bottom of the trough, while one stood guard, against what they were not sure, but Moss insisted that they take it in turns to watch out for the unexpected.

During his watch, Kel was sick twice over the side of the trough, the random rocking motion when not doing anything active, proving too much for his senses.

It was a sorry crew which greeted the dawn. Tired, disillusioned and far from everything they knew, they set to tidying up their stores, which had been redistributed by the rocking motion of the trough during the night.

They ate their first meal of the day with little enthusiasm, washed down with a small amount of their precious water supply, and after Moss had checked that the Direction Pointer was still indicating the correct direction, took up the paddles and hoped for the best.

The Greater Sun had only climbed one quarter the way up to its highest point, when Kel gave a cry of alarm.

'Oh no, look over there.'

Several long grey shapes were cleaving the water, keeping pace with the slowly moving trough.

'There are some on this side too.' Moss called out, a touch of ill concealed panic in his voice.

'Now what do we do? We can't stab that lot with the staves, and they're so big, at least ten times as long as we are tall.'

'They are much bigger than you see,' Jay added, 'some of them is still under the water.'

'Stop paddling for a while, perhaps they'll go away.' called Moss, as this was the only thing he could think of.

But the huge creatures didn't.

They all sat in the bottom of the trough, peering over the side as the huge grey creatures came ever closer.

One of the giant grey shapes left the main pack and glided over to the trough, giving it a nudge with its long snout, rocking the trough alarmingly.

Moss reached for his stave, but Jay called out,

'No, they mean no harm, they friends.'

'How can you tell that?' Moss still had the stave held at the ready, in case the huge creature tried to hit the trough again.

'They say they help us. They like us. They know where we go.' Jay was almost hysterical in her efforts to stop Moss attacking the long streamlined shape which was now gently gliding alongside the trough.

Tears began to stream down Jay's face as she saw how things could go so terribly wrong, and pleaded with Moss,

'They tell me they help us. They want to help. They like us.' She didn't know how to tell the others how she knew.

'I've not heard a word from them, so how can you?' asked Kel, trying not to sound too unkind.

'With some creatures I can do this, they tell me in pictures, I see them in my head, I tell them in pictures too. They are our friends.' Jay was beside herself in her efforts to explain the unexplainable. She knew what she meant, but didn't have the words to express it.

'All right,' said a somewhat disbelieving Moss, 'how can they help us?'

'I find out.' replied Jay, leaning over the side of the trough and sliding her hand along the flank of the huge sea creature.

It seemed to respond to her gentle touch, arching it's smooth back up and down sensually, and then with a flick of it's tail, turned away to join the others who had moved in a little closer.

Jay looked a little hesitant for a moment, not wishing to be too clever, then plucking up what courage she had left, said 'We make a loop on two of our vine lengths and tie them onto the front of the bot, they take the loop and pull us to where we want to go.'

'I don't believe this.' said Moss, the first touch of sarcasm showing in his voice.

'We don't have anything to lose,' Kel exclaimed, 'if they wanted to hurt us, we would all be filling their stomachs by now, let's give it a try.'

Two vines were made ready, a large loop being formed on the end of each, and the other end made fast to the front of the trough.

'Now what?' asked a still somewhat sceptical Moss.

'Throw them over the front of the bot, and see what happens.' replied Jay, her voice having returned to its normal gentle tone.

As the two vines hit the water, two dolphins left the pack and ran their noses into the loops. Gently pulling ahead, they took up the slack, and then the trough surged ahead as the huge tails swung to and fro.

As the trough gathered speed, a bow wave began to form at the front end, threatening to swamp the occupants with its spray. Before they could cry out, a smaller dolphin swerved over in front of the blunt ended trough, positioning itself such that it formed a streamlined shape to cleave the water, and the spray quickly disappeared, the trough surging ahead as its resistance to the water decreased.

One by one, the other dolphins who were not engaged in pulling the trough, came alongside to have their backs scratched by Jay, Kel joining in on the other side a little hesitatingly at first, and then getting quite enthusiastic about it when he realized they were harmless, and enjoyed it.

Moss meanwhile, was holding himself somewhat aloof from the proceedings, pretending to busy himself readjusting the provisions, but keeping an eye on the others, just the same.

He finally succumbed to the inevitable when both of the towing dolphins slipped back from their nooses, while another pair slid up alongside and ran their noses into the loops, and took up the strain. There was no noticeable change of speed as the change over took place, and Moss had to admit, albeit to himself, that there was some sort of benign intelligence involved here somewhere.

The trough sped on, and the Greater Sun having passed its high point in the sky, began to fall towards the horizon. The crew, with little else to do except scratch the back of the odd dolphin who came alongside, rested, giving their tired muscles a chance to recover, although Kel insisted his would never be the same again.

Moss, unknowingly took up the offered bait, fell into the trap, and a long but friendly argument ensued, much to the amusement of Jay, who had never seen anything like it.

They had expected their helpers to rest when the Greater Sun sank below the water, but as the Lesser Sun rose, it was evident that a night shift had taken over, and the trough surged on across the sparkling silver sea, leaving behind it a foaming phosphorescent wake to the delight of Jay, who thought it was very pretty, and it was a shame that it couldn't be seen during the time of the Greater Sun as well.

Four times the Greater Sun rose and sank, the trough never faltering once in its race across the ocean. Moss kept checking with the Direction Pointer to see if they were still on the indicated course, and was amazed to find that the dolphins had a better sense of direction than he had imagined possible.

On the fifth day, they saw a plume of dark smoke on the horizon, and as they drew nearer, flames could be seen lighting up the base of the huge column of smoke and ash.

Lightning darted about in the upper cloud levels, adding a deep crackling noise to the dull roar of the volcano as it spewed forth a constant stream of molten rock into the sea, building yet another island in the midst of an otherwise featureless spread of water.

While Moss and Kel were discussing what they thought it was all about, Jay interrupted their conversation,

'Our friends say there are many fire lands like that, and some of them are under the water, below us. They say the ground under the water is so hot, it runs like water, and that is what is coming out of the top of that one over there.'

'If you can talk to them,' Kel said, indicating one of the dolphins, 'why can you not talk to me in the same way?'

'I never try. I try now?' she asked, raising her eyebrows.

'Yes, all right. I'll think of something, and you see if you can see what it is.' Kel was interested, but doubted if anything would come of it.

'You think of a man like you, but older, much older. He your friend. You like him a lot. He stands by a black hole in a tree.' her eyes opened wider than Kel had ever seen them do before, even in fear.

'The tree is soo big. No tree can be so big, it would fall over.' the look of astonishment left her face to be replaced by a grin.

'You make fun of me! No place like that really.' she added, still grinning.

'Oh yes there is,' said Kel seriously, 'we both come from there, and I now believe you can see me thinking, otherwise you couldn't have seen the tree home of Mec, our Story Teller.'

Moss had suddenly taken an interest in what was going on, as he could see the possible outcome of such a gift.

'Can you see what I think?' asked Moss, screwing his face up in concentration.

'No, I not see your pictures. It is not easy to see Kel's pictures, but easy to see our friend's pictures.' she said, sweeping her arm out over the sea.

Moss was relieved that his private thoughts couldn't be eavesdropped on, while Kel didn't mind one bit. He tried to get Jay's pictures, but made no headway at all, and both were disappointed at the outcome.

Early the following day a new shape of colossal proportions joined them, and for a while the men were frantic with worry until Jay explained that the black and white killer whale would be acting as a guard on this part of the journey, for the dolphins told of a strange new creature which had been seen locally, and it attacked just about everything it came across.

By now, Moss was accepting everything about the dolphins told to him via Jay, and joined in wholeheartedly in the lookout for the new threat to their survival.

On the eleventh rising of the Greater Sun, and with their rations dangerously low, Jay announced that they would reach landfall before the Lesser Sun rose.

As there was nothing in sight except more water, they could only take her word for it, but hoped she was right just the same.

'You know, without your friends, we would have perished by now.' Moss said, looking at the only remaining water bag, and that was only half full.

'We should thank them, and that includes me,' he added.

'I told them already,' Jay said sweetly, 'I thought you want me to.'

Momentarily, Moss wondered if she really could see his thoughts, dismissing the idea, as a more comfortable option.

Low on the horizon, a faint smudge appeared, growing more distinct as they sped on through the day. By early evening, towering snow capped mountains could be seen high above the massive cliffs and hills which formed the edge of the new land they were to visit.

Jay said that it would be wise to wait until the Greater Sun had risen before trying to make landfall, as it was not an easy place to reach.

They had one last meal on board the trough, drank the last drop of water all bar a mouthful each saved for the morning meal, and settled down for the time of the Lesser Sun, guarded by Jay's flotilla of friends.

They slept well that night, and were well refreshed next morning when a gentle nudge from one of the dolphins signalled that it was time to move in closer to the cliffs.

They were towed in until they had almost reached the actual cliff face, and then the lead dolphins dropped the vines, and another pair came up behind the trough, gently nudging it into a deep cleft in the rock face. As they went deeper into the cliff, the natural light began to fade, to be replaced by a gentle glow from the surface of the cleft, mainly coming from some strange moss like marine growth.

'How much further in do we have to go, and how will we be able to get up to the cliff top from here.' asked Moss, beginning to get a little worried.

'They know this way well, it is not far now.' Jay replied, obviously still in contact with her friends.

The trough was nudged round a bend, scraping the sides of the natural split in the rock, the noise of metal on stone setting their teeth on edge for a moment, and then they were in free water again.

Six:
The Island

JUST AHEAD OF the craft was a long ledge of stone, and leading up from it were steps, winding their way up into the darkness above.

As the craft ground up against the stone jetty, the dolphins held it in place while the crew scrambled ashore, Moss passing their possessions across the bobbing side of the trough as the gentle swell of the ocean reached into the underground fissure.

'I think we should tie it up, just in case we should ever have to leave here.' Moss suggested, and did so, making the vine fast to a handy projection of rock on the quay side.

'This isn't all the work of nature.' Kel called, his voice echoing around the huge cavern. 'I think the giants had a hand in it by the size of those steps.' It wasn't until they had picked up all their equipment and actually reached the steps, that they realized just how big they were.

'We shall have to help each other up these, for if we slip and fall, that would be the end of us.' Kel said, trying to heave himself up the first one.

Jay had said goodbye to her friends, telling them where they hoped to go, and why, but was saddened by their parting as she felt she had an affinity with them which was just as strong as the one she had for Kel, but of a different nature.

The luminous growth on the walls of the cleft gave them just enough light to make their climb in reasonable safety, but they were dismayed by the effort required and the seemingly never ending steps.

Kel called a halt part way up, as he was out of breath, and assumed that the others would be as well.

'I could do with a good drink.' panted Moss, as he hauled up the larger of the equipment sacks, and tried to get his breath back.

Jay paused a moment, then handed him a small water bag, 'There one mouthful each. It got left behind when we leave the bot.'

Moss couldn't make out how anything could have been left behind. Taking the bag, he then changed his mind and said,

'You take the first drink, you have earned it.'

They continued on up the steps, the light being a little fainter now as the conditions on the walls of the cleft must have been less favourable to the luminous growth, and their main fear was that it would die out altogether before they reached the cliff top.

At last the steps came to an end, and so did the light giving moss on the walls. They were just about able to see a tunnel heading back into what they assumed to be the direction of the cliff, but they couldn't see very far into it.

'Is there any water left?' asked Kel, wishing he hadn't drunk his portion earlier on.

'A small mouthful.' answered Jay, passing the bag across to Kel.

'Where do you keep getting the water from?' asked an astonished Moss, 'I thought we had drunk it all long ago.' She didn't reply.

Kel went back to the edge of the steps where there was a little more light, and rummaged about in one of his equipment bags. Withdrawing the transparent insect case from its pouch, he tipped the last of water from the bag into it, added a small portion of the two magic powders Mec had given him, and shook it up.

A soft glow appeared in the case, and then a pale violet light began to shine out from it, and they could see quite well as their eyes had by now got used to the darkness of the foreboding tunnel ahead.

'I don't know how long it will last, so we had better hurry.' he said, and with that they picked up the few things they had laid down earlier, and almost ran down the tunnel.

The floor of the passageway began to slope upwards, and they were soon out of breath as the incline grew even steeper, and then the light pot began to fade again.

'There really is no more water now,' cried Jay, 'what we do now?' The fear in her voice spread to Moss and Kel, who were not usually frightened so easily.

'I'll shake it up a little.' said Kel, remembering what Mec had told him to do, and the light brightened up a little, but they knew it wouldn't last for long.

They raced on as best they could, but the light was fading again, and they came to a halt for fear of falling down a hole or what ever else the inky blackness held.

'I can only think of one thing, and that may not work,' said Kel, 'I'll use my water. Quick Moss, hold out your hands and I'll put a little of the powder in each, you tip it into the pot when I tell you.'

Fumbling about in the near dark and trying to direct his water into the light pot, could have been humorous if it hadn't been for the desperate situation they were in.

The light giving chemicals in the little pot swirled around as Kel did his best to fill it, and in doing so gave a gentle violet glow to the scene.

'I think that's enough, tip the powders in now Moss, and we'll see if it works.'

Moss could just about see the outline of the pot in the encroaching darkness, and managed to get most of the powders into the pot, Kel put the bung in and shook it up.

A few seconds later and the whole tunnel was lit up in the bright glow from the transparent insect case.

'It works even better than ordinary water,' Kel exclaimed,

'We must remember to tell Mec about this when we get back home.'

'Do you really think we'll ever get back to Mec and the others?' asked Moss. 'I somehow doubt it.'

Now able to see their way clearly, the trio set off at top speed up the tunnel, their footsteps echoing strangely as though there were many more of them racing along.

They almost missed the side tunnel, with its flight of steps going up again, and would have done so if Kel hadn't bumped into Moss as he slowed down for a moment.

'Now which way do we go?' asked Moss, usually the one to make the decisions.

'Up the steps again, I suppose, as we want to get out of these tunnels and into the open.' replied Kel, turning into the new passage.

The long climb up finally terminated in yet another passage, with a gentle upwards slope. Rounding a bend, they were confronted by a total blockage.

'What do you think it is? It's certainly not stone by the look of it.' Kel ran his hand over the huge steel door, some of the rust flakes coming off on his hand.

'It's not stone or wood, so it may be some kind of meetel used by the giants who made this place.' Moss said, as he pushed forward to inspect the barrier.

Moss too found the rust flakes coming off when he touched the door, and instinctively gave it a jab with his bladed stave. A small shower of brown rust rattled to the floor of the tunnel, and Moss then energetically went to work on the door as if their lives depended on breaking through, which of course they did.

Before long, there was a big pile of rust at the base of the door, and then the stave broke through into open air, and light trickled in through the tiny hole.

With Moss and Kel hacking away at the crumbling remains of what was supposed to have been an impenetrable barrier, an opening was soon made, enabling them to crawl out into the open and the bright light of the Greater Sun, which they had feared they would never see again.

'Look how thick this barrier is,' commented Kel, 'it's almost as thick as my head is wide, so why didn't they make it out of something stronger?'

'I expect it was, but over the long amount of time since it was made, it has rotted into this crumbly stuff, and just as well for us that it has!' Moss added gratefully.

They were out on an open plain of grassland which ran down to the cliff through which they had just come, and behind them were the shaggy contours of a mountain range, capped with snow and sparkling in the bight light of the sun.

The entrance to the tunnel had been carved into a small cliff which ran back into a larger rock formation of massive jumbled stone blocks.

'The first thing to do is to find some water, my throat feels as though it has been filled with dry wood scrapings.' Kel suggested, so they picked up their equipment and headed up the slope towards the rocks.

The grass was lush, and several bushes bearing fruits which looked familiar were dotted about the plain, so Moss reasoned that water couldn't be far away, and the rock pile proved his point.

As they drew nearer the jumbled cascade of stone, Jay, well out in front, waved her arms wildly and called out excitedly 'Look, water, coming down from up there.'

Above the rocks, the lip of a higher plateau jutted out, and from its edge a small stream of silver white water poured over and chattered its way down over the broken remains of a once huge water cistern.

Only the remains of the base section had survived the ravages of time, and that had filled up with water from the small stream which trickled down from above, to overflow from a crack high in its outer wall into the ground below, to disappear from view.

They quickly climbed the lower blocks, and sliding down between two massive chunks of broken concrete, reached the water's edge.

'Let's check it out first.' Kel remembered the surprise they all had from the volcanic pool on the mainland, and didn't want a repeat of that experience.

They probed the nooks and crannies around them with the staves, but nothing unpleasant appeared, and the rest of the pool looked clear right down to the bottom.

'Rinse the water bags out well, or the water will lose it's sweetness before long.' Moss called out, scooping water greedily into his mouth from cupped hands.

Having slaked their not inconsiderable thirst, and filled the water bags, Jay set about looking for an enclosed section of the pool in which she could safely bathe.

'What are you looking for?' asked Moss, always keen to know what was going on.

'I want to wash the stickiness from me.' she replied.

It was only then that Moss and Kel realized that they too were feeling unclean.

'I think it must be something from the splashes we got from the Great Water we crossed, as it tastes the same when I lick my arm.' Kel suggested, making a face which showed his disgust at the taste.

'This looks a good place.' Jay's faint voice echoed up from between the huge blocks, and the other two scrambled in what they thought was the correct direction to see what she had found.

In one corner of the huge cistern, some blocks had fallen to form an enclosed section of water, and in it was a delighted Jay, splashing about and sending a silver shower of water droplets high into the air as she cavorted about.

'This very good.' she called joyfully, and turned to splash Moss and Kel as they too entered the bathing pool.

Having removed the encrusted salt from the fine hair of their bodies, the trio returned to the grass covered ground below the old cistern to run about and dry themselves off, having discarded their carry belts and feeling free from stress and worry for the first time since beginning their long journey.

When finally exhausted, they lay down on the soft grass of the plain to soak up the warm radiance from the Greater Sun, their bodies having been chilled due to the evaporation of the water.

'I think the giants had made the water pool for their own use,' said a slightly drowsy Moss, 'because some of the big stones had flat smooth surfaces, and they don't come about naturally. There may be other remains here, left over from the earlier time, and I think we should look for them as they may tell us a little more about the giants.'

Jay agreed, adding that they may also find some things which might come in useful, and anyway, finding new things was good fun. But Kel stated that he was quite happy to lounge around for a while, and enjoy the new freedom they had found.

That evening when fruit gathering, another of Jay's talents became apparent when she stopped Kel from eating what he though was a fruit similar to those he had known in the forest.

'Not good, make you sick.' she said, taking it away from him and throwing it as far away as she could.

'How do you know that?' he asked.

'I always know what good to eat, you not know that?'

He shook his head, and Jay became their food selector by default and was to save their lives many times over.

A plentiful supply of fruit, berries and pods of various sizes and shapes, together with their water supply, satisfied their daily needs. So before long, they were looking for something exciting to do, as life was becoming a little tame after all they had shared together.

The tumbled concrete blocks of the water cistern had been gone over thoroughly and nothing other than it being the remains of a water storage unit was found, much to their disappointment.

Moss reckoned there should be the remains of the 'Giant's Hutts' somewhere about, and eventually they found the outline of a building protruding from the surrounding ground, very much weather worn, but definitely of man's construction.

'The giants must have been very much bigger than us.' commented Jay, the others nodded sagely.

'There must be something left around here, apart from their hutts.' Moss said, frustration sounding in his voice.

'They made the steps in the tunnel we came up through. Oh! and there's the other tunnel we didn't explore when we came out onto the plain.'

'I don't fancy going down there again.' Kel was quite adamant and Jay agreed with him.

Moss could see he wasn't going to get the other two down into the cliff passageways just yet, but he would try again later.

'Well, let's explore the rest of this land, there must be something else for us to find.'

Setting out next day, Moss checked the Direction Pointer and found that it had swung around to point at the mountains.

'I don't understand this,' he muttered, 'when we were in the bot, it pointed off to one side of this land, and now it has changed to point over there.' indicating the distant snow capped rocks.

'Perhaps it thinks we should go there.' offered Kel.

'It can't think!' Moss exclaimed, 'It's only a piece of twig like stuff on a piece of floating wood. Anyway, Mec said it would always point in the same direction, and now it doesn't, so we can't trust it any more.'

'Well, let's go in that direction anyway, and if we find nothing of interest, we can come back and try another way.'

Kel was impatient to carry on, there was usually something to find.

They left the flatter area of the plateau, and the gradual climb up to the foot of the mountain range began. The going was quite good, but the grass was a little coarser here with a few rocks to circumnavigate, otherwise they made good progress.

'It feels a lot colder up here, do you think we are going into the strange land of hard water which Mec told us about?' asked Kel, but Moss didn't really know either, and as he was so far up ahead, could be forgiven for not hearing correctly, as he just grunted.

So far, there had been no predators or other unpleasant surprises during their time on the island, but they still kept an eye out for the unusual, as nature had a trick of catching the unwary in a very unforgiving way.

Two days travel took them to the first sign of snow, little patches of it unmelted where it had fallen in the shadow of a rock or gully, and where the sun hadn't quite reached it.

'There you are! Hard Water.' said Kel, pointing triumphantly, and then running over to the patch of snow with Moss hard on his heels.

'I wouldn't call this hard water, Kel. It's more like soft white water, and very cold. Now this is hard water.' he said, braking off a small icicle which had formed on the edge of a rock, but soon dropped it as the chill bit into his fingers.

'If we go any higher, we shall become like that hard water, stiff and cold, so where shall we go now?' asked Kel, shivering slightly, the hairs on his body all stiffened out, trying to conserve heat.

Before Moss could answer, or a joint decision be made, the matter was taken out of their hands.

Unnoticed, a large black cloud had swept in from the sea, and they could see the sheets of rain descending from it and drenching the plateau below.

All three looked around for shelter, Jay being the first to signal she had seen something. Pointing up the slope to a sheer rock face which barred their way, a dark hole promised the chance of shelter, if they could get there in time.

The mad scramble for the cave caused much laughter later on, but at the time it was deadly serious, as the rain had turned to snow at this altitude, and felt very cold indeed.

All three rushed into the cave entrance as a single body, taking it in turns to brush off the considerable amount of snow which had already coated their back and shoulders.

'I don't like that stuff,' Jay said, snuggling up to Kel for warmth, 'I like the warm down below.'

'Me too.' the other two responded in unison.

They watched, fascinated, as a thick blanket of snow quickly built up outside the cave, and changed the entire look of the landscape.

The snow storm passed as quickly as it had come, but the clouds grew blacker and more menacing, until the first flash of lightning and the resounding crash which followed, made them jump several paces further back into the cave.

Several more strikes followed in quick succession, and they soon lost their fear when they realized that the lightning was consistently hitting the rocks some distance away.

Peering out from the entrance, Moss was the first to notice that the strikes were being attracted to a series of shiny spikes which seemed to have grown out of the very rocks themselves.

'Why don't they burst into fire like the trees did back in the forest?' he asked no one in particular. But no one knew.

Kel made the next discovery, but not its significance.

'Look at that, the last strike came down and then went sideways, as if the shiny spike wanted to be touched by it. And there's another, doing the same thing.'

'I'll bet they were made by the giants before they went away.' Moss said, a real note of confidence in his voice. 'Perhaps they could collect the sky fire, and use it for something.' he added, but without the firmness of his former statement.

Little did they know how near the truth they were.

It was ironic, and very sad in a way, that the three were witnessing man's last and most successful attempt yet to harness the power of nature without creating an overwhelming amount of pollution and problems for future generations.

The lightning attractors had been made from the finest materials available, and consequently had stood the test of time, drawing the huge amounts of energy deep down into the mountain where it was stored and converted into a more useful and manageable form.

The energy conversion and storage system had carried on working flawlessly ever since man's greed and hatred of his fellow men had caused nation to rise up against nation, both rattling their sabres, and neither willing to back down.

Eventually, someone coughed or sneezed in the wrong place, and because things were on such a fine knife-edge, it all got out of hand, and mankind, as such, was no more after the time of the Great Lights.

The lightning ceased to crackle and roar around the mountain top, the clouds lightened, and finally drifted away, while the Greater Sun came forth and bathed the whole area in its warm and comforting rays.

They stood outside the entrance of the cave, soaking up the gentle warmth, and feeling better by the minute.

'Can we see how far we go into the cave? asked Jay, and that surprised them both.

'Don't see why not,' Kel answered, 'I don't want to use the light pot unless we really have to, as I can't replace the magic powders given to us by Mec, but we could go in until it is too dark for us to see.'

When they had stopped shivering, the little group turned and went back into the dark opening. There was a fair amount of debris, small stones, leaves and the odd few twigs lying about just within the entrance, but as they went further in, it became evident that the smooth stone floor of the cave had been cut from the living rock, and was obviously not an accident of nature.

Their eyes adjusted to the falling light level as they went deeper into the side of the mountain, but they sensed that they couldn't go much further. They were just on the point of returning to the outside world because it had become too dark to see safely what lay ahead, when the titanium quartz lamp switched itself on, having detected the presence of a warm body within it's sensor range.

Their basic instinct was to turn and run, but Moss held them back from their intended headlong rush to things more familiar.

'It's only a light,' he yelled, 'like Kel's light pot, but different. Let's see what happens next.'

Nothing did. They stood there in the now brightly lit tunnel, facing a huge shiny metal door, baring their further progress.

'It's like the meetel barrier we found in the tunnel from the Great Water, but this one is made of a different meetel, like the bot we used, as it hasn't rotted like the one in the tunnel.' Moss felt quite confident in his appraisal of the situation.

Kel moved forward to give the door a thump with his clenched fist, and the deep boom which followed didn't frighten them as much as what happened next.

The door sensor mechanism circuit had partly corroded, disabling the recognition system, so that it now 'recognized' any warm bodied creature within its sensor field, and that included the three.

A soft click followed by a quiet whirring sound, and the door glided back to reveal the continuance of the brightly lit passage even further into the mountain.

'Do we go in?' asked a rather nervous Kel.

'Why not? we've come this far, and we want to find out what the giants have left behind.'

'What if we go in, and can't get out again?' Kel was only being cautious.

'All right, let's play it as safely as possible. One of us goes in, and if the barrier shuts and won't open from the inside, we can still open it from out here.' Moss was getting a little impatient, and wanted to get on with the exploration of the mysterious tunnel.

Moss bravely passed through the inviting open doorway and into the tunnel beyond, Kel and Jay, without really knowing why, stepped back a few paces, and the door hissed shut.

Kel was about to move towards the door when Jay's restraining hand held him back.

'Let Moss have a chance to open it from inside.' she said quietly.

They stood there for what seemed like ages, and then the door opened again, a grinning Moss standing just inside.

'There you are, just as I thought, we can go in and out quite safely. Come on, lets see where this tunnel goes.' and he turned and strode off down the passage, a noticeable swagger in his footsteps.

By the time Kel and Jay had plucked up enough courage to follow Moss, he had disappeared from sight around a bend in the tunnel, and they had to run to catch him up.

As they progressed down the passageway, the lights behind them went out, other lights coming on ahead of them to illuminate their way. Before long, they were taking it in their stride as they went ever further into the deeply buried Radio Telescope complex.

For a very long time the complex had been seeking out any sign of radio activity in deep space, and whenever the circuits considered a signal had been located, it sent out its own signal in the same direction.

The whole system had been set up to work automatically, powered by the lightning converters, and had done so faultlessly since it had been first constructed.

There was no way of knowing if the signals sent out had been received by anyone, until a reply came in, nor did the complex really care, it just did what it had been set up to do, and kept doing it.

Seven:
The Contact

SOMETHING, SOMEWHERE, DEEP in the Milky Way galaxy, had picked up the signals from earth, decided they were not just random transmissions from a pulsar and relayed the data forward for evaluation.   A reply was sent, and the long wait began as the series of electromagnetic pulses sped across the intervening space to Earth.

The Radio Telescope received the reply, recognized it as being a response to its original message, and sent back an acknowledgement. It didn't understand one electron of the message it had received, it didn't need to.

Messages flashed back and forth to the planetary base, decisions were taken, the great ship turned on its axis and began its long journey to a faint star on the rim of the galaxy.

✳ ✳ ✳

The tunnel down which the three had gone terminated in a large hall. From this, many doors lead to other passageways and in turn to many other rooms.

The first few doors Moss tried to open, wouldn't. Some had restricted access, not recognizing Moss or the others as approved entrants, or the selection mechanisms had broken down over the intervening years, and would admit no one.

One door did open to Moss's endeavours, and they all passed through its portal to gasp in amazement at the room's contents.

Pictures around the walls showed the giants at work and play, huge constructions in glittering steel and stone adorned the otherwise tranquil scenes of the countryside, but a countryside totally unfamiliar to the three.

A series of bench tops jutted out from the walls, and these displayed various pieces of equipment in varying stages of decay, corrosion and general breakdown of materials not designed for extreme longevity.

Few were recognizable to them, let alone the uses to which they would have been put, but at long last there was irrefutable proof that the giants had existed, and built many wonderful things as the legends had stated.

A few tools in a crumbling toolbox had survived, and Moss gathered these up not knowing what they were for, but convinced that he could put them to good use one day.

Returning to the main hall, they found two more doors which yielded to their efforts, one led down to the power room, but a strange smell assailed their nostrils as they were about to enter the enormous cavern. Jay didn't recognize the odour of ozone, but pleaded with Moss and Kel not to go any further into the place,

'It dangerous here, I feel it.' was all she would say, and they retreated back up the stairs to the hall.

Moss was keen to explore until he dropped from fatigue, but the other two were soon bored with the overwhelming non comprehension of what they saw, and wanted to return to the more pleasurable grass clad plateau by the old water cistern.

Most of the snow had melted by the time they got back to the cave entrance, and it was decided to return to the lower levels of the plain and make their main camp by the remains of the water cistern they had found earlier.

At Moss's insistent request, they returned to the Radio Telescope complex twice more over the next few days, discovering several more accessible rooms much to Moss's delight, but Kel and Jay had little interest in looking for things they could see no use for.

Before long, Moss started visiting the complex on his own, and as time went by he became more and more withdrawn and sombre in his attitude towards the others, not that they seemed to mind very much.

Nature was beginning to take a firm hand with their hormones and Kel and Jay were becoming inseparable.

Jay's natural instinct to find food which was safe for them all to eat added several new items to their diet, their health and general well-being improving beyond all measure.

A crude shelter was constructed in among the jumbled concrete blocks of the water cistern to provided a reasonable form of protection from the torrential rain which swept in from the sea every few days, although sometimes they just cavorted about in the downpour for the fun of it.

The thunder and lightning caused a degree of fear for Kel and Jay, and they took shelter whenever it was particularly fierce, but Moss largely ignored it, as he realized that most of it was collected by the lightning attractors high up on the mountainside, and therefore wouldn't affect them at this low level.

The time came when nature decided to take a hand in the proceedings, and Jay became even more attentive to Kel's wishes.

Snuggling up to him one cold night, the inevitable happened and next day a completely unabashed Kel remarked, 'What we did was so much better than what happened when Moss and I were with your group of females so long ago, I had no idea it could be so pleasant.' Jay just smiled, remembering how the two lads had been rushed from hut to hut in a drug induced stupor by a desperate bunch of broody females, blindly intent on changing their status to that of motherhood.

Many were the pleasurable moments shared by Jay and Kel, while Moss went about his business of exploring the labyrinth of passageways and rooms of the complex in the mountain. He showed no interest in Jay, except as another companion, and a rather simple one at that.

Moss suggested they set out to explore the surrounding countryside a little more, and later, from a high vantage point they were amazed to find they were on an island, with no other land in sight.

Kel and Moss had earlier discussed at length what they should do with regard to trying to get back to their home land, mainly in order to report to Mec, but now they realized the chances of achieving it were so remote as to be not really worth considering.

After much discussion, the general conclusion was that they were trapped on this island, and the only sensible thing to do was to start a group of their own, and as Moss said,

'That's your job. Anyway, I didn't like the last time we tried it, and I'm much more interested in what the giants have been doing in the past.'

Kel didn't bother to explain the difference between the two 'times', as somehow he didn't want to share Jay with anyone.

The gestation period was a lot shorter than expected, not that they knew a lot about the birthing process, and when in a more jovial mood, Moss made many jokes about Jay eating too many ripe fruits and filling up with wind.

The birth was without problems, and Kel and Jay were thrilled to bits with the little one, Moss merely remarking that it was a bit wrinkled and needed drying out in the light of the Greater Sun for a couple of days.

While she was still feeding the little one, her stomach began to swell again, this being greeted by more ribald comments from Moss, and a lot of tender loving care from Kel, who tried to make up for the somewhat disinterested and nonchalant attitude of Moss.

Something he couldn't understand had been worrying away at the back of Kel's mind, and it was when Jay was with her third child that

Kel took Moss to one side one day.

'Do you remember the law we had back in our groups that we mated with someone from another group, and never with one of our own?' Moss nodded, wondering what was coming next.

'Well, there must have been a good reason for that law to be enforced so rigidly, what do you think it was?' Kel asked.

Moss had no idea, or if he did, he wasn't going to offer it.

It was Jay who put Moss on the spot one day, by asking him if he would mate with her next time, as she somehow felt that was the right thing to do, but didn't know why. A rather reluctant Kel agreed with her, and between them they persuaded an even more unwilling Moss to do the honours.

Jay later confided to Kel that he was much better at 'it' than Moss, which restored Kel's feeling of manhood and partnership more than anything else she could have done.

When the twins were born, Moss was just as surprised as any of them, and tried his best not to show the interest he now felt in the double production.

A second set of twins, initiated by Moss, really put Kel's nose out, and that was the last time he was allowed to mate with Jay. At least for some time.

It mattered little really, as nature had achieved her aim of mixing the available genes up as best as possible, and time would tell if it had been done sufficiently.

It was during the arrival of the tenth birthing and the partnering up of the first, that Moss went missing. He was dearly loved by the youngsters, forever telling them tales of high adventure and mystery, despite his apparent reluctance.

The whole group searched in all the places he was known to frequent, some of the males from the first generation joining Kel to look deep within the mountain complex.

The conclusion they came to was that he had gained access to a room somewhere, and couldn't get out again.

The possibility of him being attacked by some ferocious beast was ruled out, as there were none found on the island.

Several days of looking produced no clue as to what had happened to him, and the search was abandoned, but he lived on in their memories for a very long time indeed.

✳ ✳ ✳

The Great Ship had begun its deceleration manoeuvres when the Navigation Officer went to the Captain and said, 'It would seem that we are not the only visitors to this system. There's a rather large asteroid heading in, and according to some rough calculations I've just done, it should graze the surface of the planet we're interested in, the third one in from the sun. If this is the case, it will probably increase the spin rate of the planet and strip off some of its atmosphere in passing. If it hits the planet, we have wasted our journey, but at least we'll see the biggest pyrotechnics display of all time.'

'How soon can you be certain of the exact degree of contact?' asked the Captain, clearly disappointed at the news.

'In another four or five ship hours. By then, there will be enough data to plot the course accurately, and I can advise you of the most probable outcome of the encounter.' The Captain nodded his acceptance.

The Great Ship approached the third planet from the sun, matched a stationary orbit over the island containing the Radio Telescope, and sent a vision probe down to see in finer detail what was there than was possible from the ship.

'I now have the latest figures for you,' said the Navigation Officer, 'and the news is not good for the future of the planet.

'It would seem that the asteroid will only graze the planet's atmosphere as I predicted earlier, but this will cause a great deal of secondary damage due to the extremely high stress levels in the planet's plate zones.'

'According to the readings I have just obtained, the internal forces have been building up for a long time, and only need a little nudge to set them off, and then the whole surface will be in for some very big changes.'

'How much time do we have before the event occurs?' asked the Captain.

'About four ship watches, and that leaves a very small margin of safety.'

'All right, here's what we'll do. The probe should be down there by now, so we'll take a look and see if there are any people on the site who we can rescue, and if so, we'll send down the largest shuttle we have and bring back as many as possible. We at least owe them that much for their efforts in trying to contact others.'

'I wouldn't give much hope for any other people on the surface after the asteroid's bypass, if the tidal waves don't get them, the volcanic gasses released after the continents relocate surely will,' the Navigation

Officer looked saddened at the prospect of such destruction, and so little hope of help.

The probe came in over the sea, giving a good view of the island and mountains beyond, and then slowed down to hover over the old water cistern where a large group of the hairy little people had gathered to enjoy their midday meal.

No one noticed the sleek silver craft as it slowly drifted up the plateau to home in on the vast aerial set in a valley between two mountains.

Having located and confirmed the signal source, the probe was brought down again to the plateau, and a close up of the group around the cistern was sent back to the waiting ship.

'These primitive looking people can't have been the builders of the transmitter,' the Captain said, disappointment in his voice, 'so where are they?'

'We have just done a preliminary radiation scan of the planet's surface which shows that atomics have been used rather liberally in the very distant past. The scars show up all over still, so it must have been a very heavy situation,' the Navigation Officer responded, 'perhaps these are the mutated remains of the master race which wrought so much destruction.'

'You could well be right. It won't be too much trouble to bring them up, and we may learn something from them. Would you see to it please?' The Navigation Officer bobbed his head in acknowledgement of the order.

The vision probe was recalled, and the shuttle with a full crew aboard departed for the planet's surface with instructions to round up as many of the small people as possible in the short time available.

The shuttle landed almost silently just below the brow of a small rise in the ground next to the old cistern, and the crew dispersed to encircle the group of natives, and hopefully shepherd them towards the rescue craft.

At first, there was panic. Once the initial shock of seeing the giants was over, and they were released from their paralysis, the little ones scattered, but this had been anticipated and most of them were guided back to the water cistern remains, and the crew leader speaking in a soft voice, tried to tell them why they were here.

He was wasting precious time, for they understood not one word, huddling together like frightened little animals, as the huge creature before them made strange noises.

'OK, let's get 'em aboard, they don't understand a word I'm saying, but it was worth a try. Be as gentle as you can, but get 'em in quickly.'

The circle of men tightened around the little group, and gradually they were herded towards the brow of the hill.

As they saw the shuttle a fresh wave of panic set in, and the crew only just managed to keep control as they darted about, seeking a large enough gap between the encircling crew members to run through.

One of the crew, seeing a large basket of fruits and pods, had picked it up, and this somehow had a calming effect on the small people, so several others of the crew did likewise, one of them waving the basket about as he went up the ramp into the shuttle.

Once the first two or three had been coerced to enter the ship, the others followed quickly, the ramp was withdrawn, the hatch closed, and they lifted clear.

The shuttle returned to the Great Ship in what can only be described as indecent haste, and began disgorging it's cargo of trembling visitors as the Great Ship moved out to a safer orbit, such that it wouldn't be affected by the coming events planet side, and the asteroid would pass harmlessly by.

As the asteroid approached the planet, smaller fragments which had been held close to it by gravitational forces suddenly responded to the greater pull of earth, and began their curving descent to the surface. The main body, as predicted, just grazed the atmosphere and proceeded on its way, stripping off some of the atmosphere in the process, to no doubt return one day and wreak further havoc once again on the luckless planet. It was the smaller fragments which were to cause so much damage.

Those which hit the sea caused vast tidal waves to course around the planet for days, sending up huge volumes of water high into the upper air and increasing the cloud cover on a large scale.

The land's surface was ripped open by a torrent of white hot fragments travelling at colossal speed, their energy expended in one frightening microsecond of impact.

Shockwaves travelled through the planet's crust, upsetting the delicate balance which had been on the edge of de-stressing itself for a long time, and now had been given the impetus to do so.

Volcanoes spewed forth from their fiery bellies great quantities of molten rock, and pyroplastic flows of fine particles cascaded down their sides to smother all before them. Steam, ash, and scalding hot corrosive gases escaped from their deep imprisonment to join the already billowing clouds of water vapour from the riven seas, the released aerosols would stay airborne for a very long time indeed.

All along the fault zones the earth split open to disgorge its molten interior, and where these splits occurred beneath the boiling sea, and the initial pressure had spent itself, the great weight of the ocean forced itself into the fissures to hit the molten rocks below.

The ensuing explosions must have deafened any remaining life forms, so thunderous where they, and the seas boiled afresh at this new assault.

The Great Ship got underway to vacate the solar system, leaving behind not the beautiful blue white planet of yesterday, with it's patchwork quilt of golden brown and green lands, but a seething mass of dirty grey clouds, boiling up into the stratosphere to race along in the jet stream, later to deposit it's deadly load of detritus over the tortured surface.

'I very much doubt anything except the lowest forms of life could survive that.' commented the Captain to no one in particular, and several officers on the bridge nodded in sombre agreement.

With the solar system fast receding behind them, the Great Ship ploughed on through space, gaining momentum as the Inter System Drive was cut in, accelerating almost up to light speed before using the Star Drive.

A team was set up to investigate the people rescued from the third planet, and this duly reported their findings, such as they were, to the Captain.

'They are a very simple race, and I mean very simple.' the team leader said. 'They are basically humanoid in form, especially internally, but there the resemblance ends. They have a very simple language with few words or sounds compared to us, and although we have tried to decipher some of these sounds, they are of a very much higher frequency to ours, and so far we haven't been able to make much sense of them.'

The team leader returned a little later, producing a thin information file which he presented to the Captain and said,

'In here is all the data we have managed to extract from them to date, but I don't think it will be of much use to anyone, except perhaps to enable a decision to be made as to what we will do with them. There is one interesting point, however, and that can't be confirmed fully at the moment, but it would seem that they are on a degenerative downward spiral, becoming less mature with each new generation.'

The Captain somewhat surprised, raised an eyebrow saying,

'That's most unusual, can you account for that?'

'Not really.' replied the team leader. 'The most likely reason for this would be inbreeding, and the conclusion we have come to is that they are somehow the leftovers from the race which built the device which sent the signals to us in the first place. What happened to them we don't know, but perhaps there was a great catastrophe, involving copious amounts of radiation and this caused a new mutation to appear. It is only speculation at this time, and we can't confirm it now due to what's happened to the planet.'

The Captain looked saddened and pensive for a while, mulling over the alternatives open to him, and finally said,

'I'll send the data on to Home Base, and they can make the final decision, but from what you say, there is little point in taking them to Base, so we had better look for a planet on which we can set them down and give them a chance, the poor creatures deserve that, at least.'

'One other small point,' the team leader added, 'some enterprising crew member managed to bring some of their native food aboard, and we have begun analysing it so that we can provide them with a synthetic version.' The Captain nodded his approval of the action.

The reply from Home Base came back as the Great Ship was approaching a dense ribbon of stars and their accompanying planets. The Navigation Officer brought the message up to the bridge and presented it to the Captain.

'They suggest we find a suitable planet which will support them and not interfere with any other life forms present, and leave it at that.'

'That may not be as easy as it sounds, but I'll have a search pattern set up right away.' The Captain didn't sound too hopeful of achieving this, as most planets which were capable of supporting life, already had it well established, and the introduction of a new variety would be bound to have some effect on the indigenous species.

Several suns where checked out for attending planets of a suitable nature, but nothing was found during the first sweep.

The Great Ship had by now reduced speed considerably to navigate safely between the closely packed stars and their planets.

Although she was fitted with the latest type of deflector shields, the crew always felt that little bit more vulnerable when journeying in such densely packed areas, the main reason being the danger of strikes from stray meteorites, which seemed to abound in such places.

At long last they found what they thought might be a suitable planet, and a vision probe was sent down to check the suitability for colonizing.

'As you can see it is mainly water covered, but there is a long strip of land mass with mountains and a high plateau.

A section of desert with a green belt next to the ocean looks promising, so send the probe down there so that we can see if it is habitable.' the Captain was pleased to have at last found somewhere to place his charges, and because of the size of the land mass, it probably wouldn't contain too many advanced life forms.

The probe skimmed along a few metres above the surface of the planet, sending back pictures of its journey in real time, its sensors looking for any warm blooded creatures as it went.

'The only life forms detected so far are fairly primitive, and our guests should be able to cope with them.' the team leader stated. 'Also there are plenty of trees, of a sort, which bear fruit and berries, and some strange looking bushes with pods which look very much like some of the pods brought up from our guest's home world.'

'That looks a suitable place then,' the Captain said, pointing out a small plateau beneath a high cliff, 'and it contains some caves by the look of it, so they can make their homes there, that's if they don't live out in the open. Was there any sign of habitable constructions back on their home world?' he asked, wanting to make sure he had set up the correct conditions for the small people.

'The only constructions we saw were those left over from the previous race, and they were mainly ruins. I suppose the small people could have lived in what was left of them, but as far as I can tell, they made no effort to build of their own accord.'

'All right, set them down and we'll keep an eye on them for a while. As long as there are no predators and they can find food, they should survive. While you're at it, have a few of the crew build a small enclosing wall from those rocks, and if necessary open up some of the caves, it may give them an idea of what to do for themselves when we're gone.' There was something the Captain wasn't happy about, but he couldn't think what it was.

The little group were herded back into the planetary shuttle, the ports being blanked over to save them from the terror of space flight, and the journey down to their new home began.

The Navigation Officer burst into the bridge with little ceremony, and rushed up to the Captain.

'After you approved the landing site for our guests, we sent the probe on to see what else we could find, and I don't quite know what to make of the results.'

'Well, what happened.' asked the Captain, wondering if this was something to do with the unease he had felt earlier and a search for another planet would be needed.

'We ran the probe up over the plateau just beneath the mountain range on the far eastern edge of the land mass, and found the remains of what looks like a mining operation.

'It may not have been, but there were several large buildings and a fair amount of equipment left scattered about in various states of decay. I would think it had been abandoned in a bit of a hurry by the way things were left about, and probably some time ago by the degree of corrosion on some of the equipment.

'But that shouldn't affect our friends because of the intervening desert area, I don't think they would be able to cross that.' The look of relief on the Captain's face was plain for all to see.

'I agree with that,' said the Navigation Officer, 'but something else happened. The probe was detecting a series of low level heat sources from the ground in the area near the buildings, so we lowered it almost to ground level, finally landing it to pick up some samples of the sand and small stones to check for radiation as a possible cause. The next thing we knew, the probe had been tossed up into the air, caught in something, and then we assume, crushed flat. It was certainly the end of the signals from it.'

'I don't like the sound of that,' the Captain exclaimed, 'it was just ordinary looking flat sand and stones, and it up and chewed our probe into oblivion? What do you make of it?'

'I don't know. It's never happened before, so we have nothing to go on. It can only be one of two things, a mechanical defence mechanism or some unheard of alien monster. I prefer the defence mechanism, myself.'

The Captain was thoughtful for a moment before saying,

'Whatever our probe found, it is far removed from the site we will be using for the small people, and I'm sure they couldn't get across the desert to reach the plateau, so I don't think we have anything to worry about. Just make sure there's nothing like that in the area we have chosen for them, they at least deserve a fair start.'

A second probe was sent down and the area around the chosen site was checked for any sing of the mystery 'probe destroyer', but there was no hint of any aggression towards the scouting probe.

The shuttle disgorged its payload, and the crew which had been sent to show how to build a defensive wall got to work.

The small people just looked on, whether they understood what was being shown to them was anyone's guess, but the crew followed their orders to the letter, and did their best to demonstrate the art of stonewall building.

The caves were checked out for anything nasty which might have taken up residence therein, but all was well, and after a bit of pushing and shoving, the crew managed to get some of the small people to enter a cave and not rush out again in a blind panic.

By the time the shuttle had climbed back to the Great Ship, everyone was congratulating each other on a job well done, and a degree of genuine interest in the small people had developed.

It was the general intention to orbit around the planet for a while to see how its new incumbents managed, and then report back to base for new instructions.

After five 'days' of the planet's time, and several deaths due to eating the wrong fruit, it seemed that the new locals had found out what they could eat safely, but at a price.

The team on board the Great Ship reported back to the Captain that all seemed well down below, and they prepared to leave the small people to their own devices, hoping that nature would now take care of her own.

A few rudimentary tools made by a kind engineer and left in the fond hope that some among the tribe would find a use for them, but it didn't seem likely from the response the crew got when they presented their departing gifts.

After one final check to see that all was well, the Great Ship left its orbit around the planet, accelerated out of the solar system and headed out into deep space, its primary function completed.

The tribe had lost quite a few of their number before they finally found out which fruits, berries and pods they could eat safely, but having done so, set about organizing themselves into coherent working groups, continuing to build the defence wall and cleaning out enough of the caves to house them all.

Unfortunately, long ago, Moss, Kel and Jay hadn't bothered to set up the Story Teller routine, too busy were they in propagating their numbers, and just having a good time.

There was now little of the tribe's history being passed down, so they had no idea of how they had originated, or from whom. Only recent happenings were recalled with any clarity, and they didn't seem to last very long.

Here was food aplenty for them to gather, and a supply of clean drinking water was found in a large rock cluster not far from their encampment, so their basic needs were fulfilled.

During the daylight hours, all was quiet and relatively peaceful, but the noises of the night set many a tooth on edge, and rumours were soon flying around as to what could be making such a din.

The night time screams did at least serve one useful purpose, it kept the tribe well within their compound during the nocturnal hours, as no one would dare to leave their haven and run the risk of adding to the hideous cacophony of sounds which often rent the hours of darkness.

Slowly the tribe's numbers began to build up, until there was not really enough room for them all to find sleeping quarters in the caves, so some had to sleep outside in the open. This didn't go down well after one of their number disappeared one night, and then someone remembered how the Giants who had brought them here had enlarged one of the caves by scraping at the walls with a long blade.

A blade was found among the artefacts left behind by the crew of the Great Ship, although it seemed a little smaller than the one used by the Giants.

Once the initial surface had been cut through after much effort, the softer lime and sandstone mix beneath gave easily to the hacking of the steel blade, and the newly cut surface later hardened due to the reaction with the atmosphere.

Once they had got the hang of it, cave enlargement went ahead at a great pace, and soon everyone had a retreat from the dreaded horrors of the night.

As the tribe's numbers increased still further, a form of job allocation became apparent.

The largest of them becoming guards, armed with stones and the largest sticks they could find, to protect the smaller ones from any predators which they might encounter while food collecting or going to the water pool in the rocks.

So far, no one had actually seen anything of the night beasts, but they knew they existed and were taking no chances.

It was a pity that the skills of the original three hadn't been passed on down through the generations, and a series of Story Tellers set up, but nature, for want of a better word, had a way of correcting things, no matter how badly man has messed them up.

Once she had got life started, no matter what disaster struck, some way was found, some rule bent, so that it could carry on.

And so it was to be with the small people, but a little time would have to pass before the next phase of her great work could commence.

The End

**More from sci-fi-cafe.com
by David Reynolds-Moreton**

Anthology of Futures
Anthology of Possibilities
Divergence
Enslavement
Exchange Rate
Extreme Difference
Flight of the Tristan
Fully Guaranteed
Greenways
Inheritance
Light Quest
The Martian Enigma
The Power Seeds
The Seed Garden
The Single Twin
The Sweepers
The Tribe
Transplant
Of Wood, Metal and Glass

www.ingramcontent.com/pod-product-compliance
Lightning Source LLC
Chambersburg PA
CBHW050541190726
48284CB00003B/1171